HOW TO CONTROL GRAVITY

GRAVITY

AND OTHER SECRETS TO LOVE
AND INTERSTELLAR TRAVEL

Edited By Rebecca Rutledge

Cover By Natasha Alterici

Back Cover Illustration By Don Rosencrans

HOW TO CONTROL GRAVITY

AND OTHER SECRETS TO LOVE AND INTERSTELLAR TRAVEL

By Charles J. Martin & Will Weinke

Cover by Natasha Alterici

TABLE OF CONTENTS

SO, YOU'VE LOST YOUR EDGE. NOW WHAT?

I know where creativity comes from. Specifically. I know the part of the brain that keeps alive that magical spark because I can feel its warm anxiety. Place your fingers on your temples, trace them upwards along your skull while drifting forward a half inch and your fingers will meet at the top where that spark lives. When I was young, this region raged like a lightning storm. But as I neared forty, it cooled, turning quiet, cold, and barren.

I knew the second that my roaring engine went silent. Thirty-seven years pumping fire throughout my entire body, pushing me to spend countless months poring over stories, writing, editing, tweaking, reworking, all just to chase this hope of brilliance, of perfection, of success.

That was all gone. Novels withered and were forgotten, A few novellas shuffled out into the world, emaciated and hopeless, but soon all I could hope for were short stories with near horizons and a few editorial sweeps before I kicked them out the front door.

I didn't even read the same. I didn't attack the stories, scaling them one foothold at a time as I pulled myself to their summit. Instead, I trudged up a few steps, shrugged and turned back for home. I was in full mid-life crisis mode and left with two options: panic or give up.

I chose to panic.

I put myself on a rigid workout regimen. I tried to rein-sert myself into the indie rock scene. Last month, I forced one of my gay friends to go shopping with me so I could learn how to dress younger. Less aging, professorial, failed novelist type and more neo-Peter Pan in a clever t-shirt and carefully-aged Converse.

Also, my girlfriend was twenty years old. She was brilliant, one of the smartest people I've ever known, but she resented dating someone so old; she resented me for dating someone so young. Still, we laughed a lot and she made me feel more vital. It was a doomed relationship, of course. But it was fun.

For the record, I am four years younger than her dad.

All this to explain why, when I drove past the billboard asking "So, You've Lost Your Edge. Now What?", I was primed to buy into whatever snake oil they were selling. I am not a billboard guy. I don't know that a billboard has ever sold me on anything aside from the next opportunity to relieve my full bladder on a long road trip.

But I was a writer who'd lost his will to write, so I was desperate. The black billboard with simple white lettering only accompanied the pressing question with a phone number.

I drove past the billboard, considered, shook off the curiosity, then changed my mind, exited, and looped back around. I hated myself for it, but, as I mentioned, I was in full mid-life crisis mode. Also, I am a sucker for a weird time.

I made the call while my car idled on the side of the highway, like some depraved john hiding his shame from the family. I was greeted on the second ring by a munching sound. I could hear football playing on a distant television.

"Hello?" I asked.

More munching. I guessed he was eating nacho cheese-flavored tortilla chips or something equally crunchy and obnoxious.

"9 p.m." The man's voice was curt, deep, and phlegmy.

"Tuesday, Exit 453 off I-40, three miles south, turn left at the stupid barn, look for lights and cars."

"Sorry, is this the place that—"

"You've lost your edge, right?" the man asked. More crunching. "Exit 453 off I-40, three miles south, turn left at the stupid barn, look for lights and cars."

"What is it that you do?"

"Look, Will," the man said. "Just show up."

"How do you know my name?" I asked, but the line was dead.

I would spend the next three days obsessing over what I should wear to a clandestine meeting in the middle of nowhere that strongly implied the recovery of my edge, but more likely would lead to my gruesome homicide at the hands of a band of depraved hillbillies with a perplexing appetite for middle-aged men.

I decided on my new trendy blazer, black skinny jeans, a Shropshire Plaid t-shirt, and Converse with "Who Will Save Us From Wonderboy?" painted on the sides.

***

"But how did he know my name?" I whispered three hours before the meeting while at my writing partner's house, his kids sitting around a half-finished game of Risk while we stood just out of earshot in the kitchen.

"Caller ID," Charles responded, not even looking away from the game board a room away.

"Oh," I said. "Yeah, of course. Shit, I am such an idiot."

I followed his eyes toward the board. His youngest son had overextended into North America, leaving his eastern European front vulnerable.

"Should I go?" I asked.

"If it has any chance of getting you writing again, yes," Charles said, before walking to the table and reaching between his kids to push a pile of troops from Siberia into Ural.

"I'm about to inflict the full force of Mother Russia upon the disgraceful swine you call an army and push your decadent bourgeoisie back through Germany and all the way into the Atlantic Ocean," Charles announced in one of the worst Russian accents I'd ever witnessed. "I will create a worker's paradise across the Western World."

Charles turned to me. "Russia was a communist nation by World War I, right?"

"It happened about mid-way through the war, I think."

"Excellent, I will crush all of you capitalist dogs!"

**

Of course, I knew I was going. There was no doubt in my mind that I was going, but I was still humiliated. In fact, I was even more humiliated during the drive to Exit 453 than I was when I went to the urologist to score boner pills. But I couldn't go back to a life of false starts, abandoned novels, and charmless stories.

I was a writer, I'd always been a writer. I promised myself two decades ago that once my work lost its spark, I would kill myself.

Well, my writing's vitality was sapped, yet I was nowhere near ready to kill myself. Funny how easily that goalpost can move.

The "stupid barn" was easy enough to find, as it was lit up by floodlights on all sides. The barn's God-fearing owner proclaimed his religious fervor with a mural collage of Biblical imagery such as a blonde-haired Jesus holding a lamb, a star spewing a rainbow down over the double-doors, and a winged angel toting a pump-action shotgun—all done in brazen primary colors and very poor technique. It was amazing in a Midwestern church kitsch kind of way.

On the roof, big block letters proclaimed "Demon Women Stay Away!"

It begged me to pull out my camera phone so it could be shown to the world, but I was worried about missing the "Losing My Edge" support group meeting. Or timeshare pitch. Or gang bang.

The turnoff was a dirt road. I drove another three miles before I saw lights off to the right and a pack of cars parked in a field. I pulled up behind a Dodge Ram with chrome Truck Nutz and a "Don't Blame Me, I Voted For John Rambo" bumper sticker. A Porsche was parked nearby. On the other side was a cluster of Harley Davidsons. A few other sports cars dotted the makeshift parking lot otherwise dominated by trucks. There was only one other sensible, fuel efficient family sedan like my Camry. I had an ally out there somewhere.

I emerged from my car to find that a chill had swept in during the drive from Oklahoma City. My breath showed in small white puffs. Ahead, maybe fifty yards, men stood in clusters around the portable lights set up near a grumbling generator. We were all waiting for whatever was going to give us all back the fire of youth. Some were around my age, some older. I walked across the tractor-cut grass field and stood close to the loose huddles, but just enough apart for safety's sake. Scanning their faces, I saw a lot of ex-football players with thick builds, a few country boys, and some aged club rats with even douchier blazers than mine.

"Hey," a squat, barrel-chested biker called to me. "You look like a man with answers. What the hell is going on out here?"

"I don't know, but if I start hearing dueling banjos, I'm running the other way."

The bikers laughed. I felt better. Just like in high school, get 'em laughing and everything will be okay.

A small, spectacled man in a pillowy coat approached from the fields beyond the lights. He held a clipboard and seemed the sensible sedan type. I imagined we would be friends by the end of the night. He clapped his hand against the clipboard, then whistled through his fingers.

"Attention everyone! If you could follow me!"

"Ah," the biker said. "I asked the wrong nerd."

Yup, just like high school.

We followed Other Nerd beyond the floodlights, deeper into the fields. There was some sporadic laughter, but mostly everyone ambled along, hands stuffed in pockets, looking everywhere but into each other's nervous eyes. The temperature dropped more and more as we hiked across the countryside. I glanced back at the distant floodlights and guessed at my odds of being able to sprint back to my car should the worst happen.

I'd also taken up jogging as part of my mid-life crisis action plan, so I liked my odds.

My breath came out in plumes now, my thin blazer useless against the cold. My foot slid on ice, and I flailed my arms, abandoning all elegance and integrity in a desperate attempt to stay on my feet. I steadied, then gazed ahead towards a vast, frozen lake. I stepped back off the ice, then looked to Other Nerd, who stood on the ice twenty feet off the shore. The other men were behind me, examining the spectacle. I had no idea how I hadn't noticed the lake, but I was prone to tunnel vision.

Another figure appeared from the other side of the lake, walking out across its glimmering surface. The figure was tall, thin, and traditionally handsome with a leading man jawline and a full head of hair that rustled with the wind like wheat in a field. He met us with a broad and confident smile. He was a man with edge and I was immediately ready to buy in. Other Nerd didn't turn as the tall man approached, instead watching us, silent and amused.

"Good evening gentlemen! My name is Elijah!"

A cult, I thought. I've had experience with one before, and that ended with a pile of severed hands and the disappearance of over 4,000 people. So I dreaded the possibility of getting called first.

"I apologize for the travel and the dreary weather, but this is simply how the process goes," Elijah said. "You are here because you feel depleted of your youth. Maybe you want better sex, maybe you want to work longer hours, or be an athlete again. Perhaps finish another novel."

His eyes met mine. My stomach knotted as I was reminded of Jim Jacobs. A cult leader. A maniac. My friend.

"You are ultimately all here for the same reason. To be young again. Step out onto the ice if you are serious about a new beginning and we will decide who is worthy."

All of the candidates looked down on the ice. I'd already felt its surface when I'd accidentally stepped on it. There'd been a slight give. It wasn't thick. It wasn't safe.

"We will not beg you," Elijah called. "You either step onto the ice to be judged or you turn around and leave. If you do join us but are deemed unworthy, your night will also be over, you will be no worse for the wear."

"And if we are chosen?" a voice from our herd asked.

"Then your life changes," Elijah said. "Just as mine did. The results are pure magic."

We still idled at the shoreline. The dread twisted in my guts. I thought of going home. I thought of the divorce. I thought of the twenty-year-old girlfriend. I thought of the failed career.

"Fuck," I muttered, then stepped onto the ice. I tested it for a moment, felt it sink ever so slightly, but it held. I put my other foot on the ice, took a deep breath, then crossed with caution. Elijah and Other Nerd watched me with knowing smiles.

"Good," he said, waving me forward.

I turned back to see five other men stepping onto the ice and making their way toward us. The rest stayed on the bank.

"That is good," Elijah called. "The rest of you may leave. Have a pleasant life. Do not come back to this place."

My heart swelled and hummed. I was proud. Damn proud. There weren't many victories in my life those days, so that moment felt good. To have someone impressed with me felt good.

"Stop," Elijah said.

I looked over to the other men as they walked alongside me. We waited shoulder-to-shoulder, all trying to hide our fear.

"There, that is just right," Elijah said. "Thank you for coming, all of you. Thank you for trusting us. One of you will be moving on."

"Who?" the barrel-chested biker asked.

"That's up to her," Other Nerd said.

The ice cracked and caved. I fell in before I thought to scream. The cold shocked my body. I flailed to get back to the surface, emerging between chunks of ice, slapping my hands against the slick surface, searching for a grip. I saw Elijah and Other Nerd smiling down at me. The others were backing away from the broken ice, terrified. One turned and ran back to the shore. The biker scrambled toward me.

"Leave him!" Elijah shouted, but the biker dropped to his knees, spreading out his weight, and reached a hand out for me.

Other Nerd pulled a pistol out from under his coat and leveled it on the biker.

"Leave him."

"He will be fine," Elijah insisted. "He has been chosen. Go home and never come back."

The biker stood, hands in the air. He looked back to me.

"Sorry, buddy."

He turned and ran.

I tried to pull myself back onto the ice, but the slab cracked again, tilting up in the air and sending me back down into the water. I surfaced, wading, eyes on Elijah.

"You should have dressed warmer, my friend," he said.

Below me, I felt fingers latch onto my ankle. I began to scream, but was yanked under. The water rushed over me as I reached for the ice. I dropped into the depths like I was tied to an anchor. I looked down for what held my ankle, but only saw darkness. I looked up, barely able to make out the fading moonlight shimmering through the ice. Down, down, down. Oxygen was gone. Cold invaded my bones.

Death felt near.

A glow emerged beneath me, the earth opening up on the lake bed, revealing a warm orange light. I still couldn't see what held my ankle, dragging me. The light swallowed me whole. I was certain that I'd fallen into hell.

My face smacked concrete. Pain erupted in a shower of stars and confusion. I was no longer underwater. I spasmed, gasped in air, flailed, rolled to my knees, and coughed out lake water. I focused my bleary eyes.

Metal walls all around me. Above, a deep blue ceiling yielding faint light. Doors surrounded me in three directions. I moved to a wall, pressing my back to its cold steel, comforted by its rigidity, its anchor. I looked back to the ceiling. A murky white light shimmered.

The moon shining through the frozen lake.

I was still underwater. I scanned the ceiling for a porthole, something that I could have been pulled through, but found nothing. There was no water on the ground. My clothes were dry, my hair was dry. I was neither cold nor warm, just numb.

I stood and looked from one door to the next, considering my options. This was still part of some plan, but I was certain that it had nothing to do with regaining my edge, nor scoring a 'scrip for testosterone supplements. I was a sacrifice of some kind.

"So, run, right?" I asked myself.

"Yes, definitely," I answered.

I sprinted for the middle of the three doors.

A siren erupted, blasting through the room, shredding my ear drums. I fell to my knees, clasping my hands over my ears, teeth clenched, waiting out the screaming, shrill siren. Pain drove into the center of my skull like a rusty nail.

It eased and then died, but my eardrums still rang.

"What is art?" a woman asked, her voice clear through the ring in my ears. "What is art?"

The voice was in my mind—deep, intelligent, but with a soft purr at the edges, like the first teacher I fell in love with.

I knew I needed to start moving. I needed to find a way out. With my hands still pressed against my ears, I leaned up on my knees and opened my eyes. The room was still empty.

I found my feet and straightened. I examined the three doors, considered the middle door again. The siren emerged, soft this time, like a grumble from a weary dog. I looked to the door on the right. I took a step forward, waited for sound, but nothing. I hurried across the room, pausing for a moment before reaching for the metal door handle.

I threw the door open. Water burst out, washing me across the room and smacking me against the far wall. I pushed off and spun around to the closed door.

The water was gone, my clothes were dry again. The pain in my head gone, my eardrums clear of the ring. I looked to the door on the left. It was a game, and this was their way of showing me how to play.

But I could wait it out. I could refuse to participate, sit down, force the monster to come to me. I knew this room. I knew what was in it, but that third door? The one I was being pushed toward? I had no idea what was behind it.

"What is art?" she asked again, still only in my mind.

"Communication of soul," I answered out loud.

The third door swung wide, slamming against the wall. Behind it, only darkness.

"I don't understand what's happening," I called, but

received no answer.

I walked to the door. Peered into the darkness.

"What is happening?" I said. "Answer me and I'll go through."

My nostrils caught the scent of burnt ozone, that first gasp of a struck match.

Black smoke tumbled from the door and swept across the concrete floor, engulfing my feet. There was no heat, just an illusion.

"What is art?" she asked, her voice real this time. Behind me.

I turned around to face a pillar of smoke building, taking form. Sparks flashed within.

It burst outward, unveiling a monstrous woman. The smoke formed wings that sprawled wide like a moth's. Her naked form was streaked with white, gray, and black. Round, glassy, spheres glowed like magic orbs implanted across her body. One above her hip and to the right of her womb, another near her shoulder, one in her neck, two more in her palms. Tiny dots of whites, blues, soft reds, yellows glowed within as if each orb contained miniature solar systems.

Her mouth was wide, carnivorous, and alien with every tooth a fang. Her eyes were almost human, but too wide and sharp. The kind of terrible and beautiful monster that frightens the brave, seduces the powerful, and inspires myths that outlive civilizations.

"You are going to die, Mr. Weinke," she said.

She glided across the ground, nearing me. Terror froze me in place.

"Now run!" she screamed.

And I did, sprinting into the darkness of the doorway, falling into something empty, cold, and hopeless.

"You are going to die, Mr. Weinke."

I felt no warmth in my body. I felt no breath in my lungs. I felt only regret.

Black regret. Forever black.

"This is death, Mr. Weinke."

"Why?" I tried, but no sound came from my lips.

Stars ahead of me. A circle of stars, their brightness reaching me as if emerging from a pool of ink. The circle was constrained, bigger than my body, but not by much. I could not tell how far the stars were from me. Perhaps ten feet, perhaps ten light years. My mind couldn't make sense of it.

"This is life, Mr. Weinke."

I looked within the circle of stars, seeing a yellow sun, seeing a tiny blue planet.

"Every love, every memory, every story you've told, every hand you've held, all within this life. What have you left behind, Mr. Weinke?"

I gazed at the stars, focusing on the blue planet.

"What have you left behind, Mr. Weinke?"

"Nothing," I tried, but still silence.

The stars drifted away. I reached out to them, but my weightless body spun in a flailing pirouette. I twisted, craning my head around to watch the retreating sphere, but then saw the soft flesh of an abdomen around the stars. The abdomen led to hips and a chest, a second circle of stars next to a shoulder, a third implanted in a neck, and finally I saw the head. She was a giant now, at least five stories tall. Her gaping mouth showed rows of sharp fangs, eyes black. Her arms spread wide like a welcoming lover, circles shining out of her palms.

"You do not deserve this life, Mr. Weinke. All you deserve is death and obscurity."

"Please," I tried, watching her fade from me.

"What is art, Mr. Weinke?"

"Life!" I shouted, this time finding breath.

Gravity took hold. I fell towards her, plummeting, screaming, plunging into the circle of stars in her abdomen.

Freezing water.

Ice breaking.

My body shot skyward out of the water, spinning in the air, a moment of weightlessness, then gravity caught me.

I crashed back down onto the frozen lake.

Gasping in breaths. My skin chilled, body shivering violently. Men rushed toward me; a blanket was thrown over me. I was pulled to the shore. I didn't fight, just stared at the break in the ice.

Elijah stood over me.

"You weren't good enough?" he asked.

"No," I said through the shivers.

Elijah knelt down close. He placed his hand on my shoulder.

"What do you do now, brother?" he asked.

Further down the shore, two men with torches approached the ice. They were escorting an elderly man, hardly able to walk on his own. His body trembled, not from the chill, but from the cruelty of time. Elijah stood and turned to watch them. The old man looked past Elijah toward me. He smiled weakly, then continued across the lake. The men with torches neared where I fell in, stopping just shy and letting the old man go on without them. He walked past where the ice belched me back out of the lake, several steps beyond where Elijah greeted us.

The ice broke. The old man fell into the water. Elijah smiled, whispering a prayer to himself.

The ice burst into steam. The night's chill warmed as fog rolled over me. Mist swirled, settled, cleared and revealed an empty field. No lake. No Elijah. No men. No lights. Only the first hints of a rising sun.

"What do you do now?" Elijah's disembodied voice whispered.

I took several moments to watch the world wake up around me. I pushed myself to my feet. I began my long walk back to Life.

MY HEART IS A GIANT

See the lips scarred and blistered from too many years crossing too many barren deserts. See the hobbled limp left after losing too many toes during too many fruitless climbs up frozen mountain faces.

See the mangled stump left after my poor giant gave his right hand to the Great Sea.

But also see the smile he offers to every rising sun.

I don't understand his resilient joy, but because of his size, he sees the world's glory in a way that I never can. He rises from every fall, survives every wound, and smiles to the horizon as if he'd never known pain.

And we walk on.

Don't mind his tattered shirt, his muddy shoes, his torn pants. I clothe him well because I want us to exude pretension and high breed, but I cannot keep him from rolling in the dirt with every mongrel and stray we come across. He loves dogs because they love him. Not much in this world is so unconditional, so how can I say no?

To be honest, it does me good to watch him play. He is the last of what remains of my youth. My hope. He still believes, so I watch him wrestle and laugh and frolic until he has had his fill. He jogs back to me breathless, rejuvenated. I straighten his collar, brush back his hair, tell him I am so very proud.

Then we walk on.

Collecting lovers and enemies, friends and sorrows.

He stands bravely against the predators ever flocked on distant cliffs, but startles at beauty. You know this, for he always startles at you. Despite my warnings and protests, he clambers after love, racing across miles of wasteland, dragging me behind like a toy to be thrown at love's feet. An offering in exchange for nourishment.

And we are starving.

See the dark spot upon his chest. Ugly and sick. It came from the hospital. Six months of sadness as we watched our friend wither away. That sadness infected my giant, weakened him, and marked upon him that eternal bruise. Tender and not a thing to be overcome, it is only to be suffered. In time, we would both love that spot because the pain would never let us forget. It is a comfort. At least this one thing would be forever.

It is not his only spot, but it remains the largest. More are sure to come.

Let me tell you of the Great Sea. We spent years drifting through its wondrous expanse, at times forgetting the feel of solid land. Cleansing summer showers, harrowing typhoons, storm swells as imposing as city skylines. We watched the vast waves chase us for days before overtaking and descending upon our small ship like a dark shadow consuming the world.

Many times I thought I'd lost my giant to the turbulent, churning waters, but he always found his way back. He would paddle through currents colored red by his own blood, beaming a joyful smile on his return to me.

The monster that took his hand had surfaced one night. No storm to warn us, no violent winds or crackling thunder, just an empty deck where my giant made his bed. When he surfaced later that night, he was pale and spent. It took me hours to pull his waterlogged bulk onto the deck where he collapsed without a word into a fitful, twitching sleep. I never saw the monster because I didn't want to see the monster. I never do.

Next morning we watched the sunrise together. His skin burned with fever and blood still flowed from his wound, but his smile was as happy as ever.

I asked him if it was time to find a port and escape the ocean once and for all.

Not yet, he insisted.

We sailed a few more months and tried not to speak of the monster, yet I caught him looking into the depths when he thought I wouldn't notice. I never knew what he wanted to find within the Great Sea or whether he hoped to retrieve his right hand, but once we finally made land and stepped onto the beach, my giant never looked back to the water.

We've become vagabonds since, meandering from adventure to adventure. I now understand his patterns. Loyal to what is loyal to him, but too easily confused by love. I joke often of entering the priesthood, but he never laughs.

So we walk on.

He seems capricious. I know. I won't argue, but I will ask you to understand that he just wants to believe. He is reverent and noble, but he doesn't understand life. He never will. Don't try to explain yourself, because he will only be confused and upset. When he is afraid he hides in deep caves and dangerous dark places. We disappear. We become safe far down within the earth where days and night pass as a single moment. A long, lonely, and hollow moment. It takes months to lure him back out into the sunlight.

I want to find him a home. It is time. Not another Great Sea—we've wandered those endless angry waves long enough. I've heard of meadows and modest hovels, seasons passing peacefully, years dripping by. Every morning a sunrise, every evening a glowing hearth. That is what he needs.

My heart is a giant and he still believes in you. He will run to you whenever you are near—but you are not home, are you? It's okay. You never said that you were. But perhaps it is time for you to leave.

It is time for us to walk on.

MORE DANGEROUS DEAD THAN ALIVE

My last memory of Bo Harrison was the stench of gasoline. I poured it over him. I lit the match. I took him from this world. I loved him. Professional ethics be damned, I loved Bo Harrison with the entirety of my heart. He was my patient. He was a killer. He was irredeemable, so I took him from the world."

"Why the gasoline? Why not the charred flesh? Surely that smell would be more potent."

"I don't remember smelling anything past the gasoline. My brain shut off."

And that was the truth. She didn't remember charred flesh, though she did develop a distaste for barbecue.

Dust swirled and danced, the sunlight peered in between the almost-shut blinds. The air conditioner kicked on, blowing tiny, glittering tornadoes of dust from the vents. Will's dust. She found it comforting. In his office, on his clothes, throughout his house, even on his bedsheets. Now all dust smelled of Will in her mind. They gave up sex long ago, but they still hugged when they met and with that proximity came the dust cloud settling over her.

She shifted on the leather chair, then returned her finger to the same crack she always picked at every time she visited his office. As a therapist, she understood the counseling session on a deeper level than the average client, but that didn't prevent her from returning to the tics common among all clients, tiny outlets to ease nerves or simply distract. The leather possessed dozens of cracks where clients found their own seams to call home for forty-five minutes at a time.

"I will be honest, I don't think I could have done it. I remember how happy he made you, during that brief time when you two were—well."

"Fucking?"

She loved how the word shot from her mouth. She didn't cuss often, but when she did, she made it count. Will leaned away, his old office chair squeaking at its rusty metal joints. She was certain that the word was a gutshot. No ex-lover wanted to hear about other ex-lovers in anything but the worst light. He was blushing. She savored the direct hit. He deserved it for bringing her here.

But it was also too dangerous to leave. He had her trapped.

Someone coughed in the adjoining reception office where a secretary would normally be stationed. She met Will's eyes, remembering his smile that surfaced in hard times. A strong, open smile. A savior's smile. It was nowhere to be found today.

"I was thinking 'dating' or 'in love.' Something more polite."

"You don't date your patients. You fuck them. You can't romanticize a complete violation of the client/therapist boundary. He was my only misstep in twenty-three years. Just him."

She looked up to see how the second hit impacted. Will only smiled. Not his warm, redeeming smile, but an adversary's cryptic grin. His chair rotated slightly as his feet fidgeted under the desk. She'd ease off him now. She just wanted to assert herself, show him that she wasn't powerless. No matter what the situation implied, she still had claws to scratch.

He opened her file. A manila envelope a size too small

for its thick trove of sheets. He scanned notes, just a trick to allow him time to collect his thoughts. She was goading him, he was too polished to let himself get drawn in.

"I find your phrasing interesting. 'Only misstep.' Bo might have been the only client you had sexual relations with, but not the only violation of the trust between you and your clients."

"I don't know what you are talking about, Will."

That grin again. He was rallying, like a boxer pushing himself back to his feet, punching his fists together, about to reenter the fray.

"I see. Well, tell me this: would you still have done what you did had that romance not blossomed?"

"Would I have set him on fire?"

"Correct."

"No. Probably not. I didn't kill him because I felt betrayed or anything like that. I killed him because I felt he was my responsibility. I had to be the one to either talk him down or to end him. It had to be me."

"That makes sense."

"Does it?"

"Yes. When I was a child, my father shot our family dog when it bit a girl down the street. He said that it was our job to do the right thing since he was part of our family."

The air conditioner shut off. She watched the beams of sunlight, the slow-drifting patterns they made on the cheap, institutional carpet. She moved her eyes to the family portrait, his beautiful, almost-too-young-and-hip wife. The step kids with clever, affected smiles. Then to the wall. She passed by the diplomas and settled on the staff photo from the McAlester Special Needs Rehabilitation Center. He'd survived a prison riot by hiding in his office for a week.

Will was patient. He had time. She didn't.

"Bo was not a dog."

She hated saying it, hated the pain she heard in the clipped edges of her consonants. It made her feel exposed. She looked up, hoping for the smile, knowing it wouldn't be there.

"Of course not, but you did what you felt was right. And you both became celebrities for it."

Tagged, like a right hook to the chin. She did her best not to show any emotion, but her hands folded up on her lap, her eyes went to the carpet.

"Yes."

"Let's talk about Bo a little more. He wasn't just a lover and he wasn't just a killer."

"No."

She wondered what would happen if she got up and left. Her ears reached out for sound from the reception room. In her fantasy it would be empty, the door open. She could escape. But she felt bodies in there, the heat of them, the authority they represented.

"Killing the wealthy and decadent, absorbing their opulence. The American Robin Hood, stealing from the rich and giving to himself. That is what people said. Then you wrote the book on him with that wonderful title."

"More Dangerous Dead Than Alive."

"Yes. Tell me about the title. What does it mean to you?"

Eyes still on the floor, ears still trained on the adjoining room. The men had arrived after she did. She'd heard them behind her as she dashed up the steps to Will's office. It seemed like they'd been just out of sight, shadowing her steps for days now.

She heard a mumble. Male. Deep. She pictured a brute, a bruiser, like the kind that roughed up Humphrey Bogart for getting too close to the truth. Or the unhinged detective who knew how to dive into dark, dangerous alleyways and emerge, bloodied and spent—but with answers.

"Sharon?"

"Don't call me that. I've always hated that name. You know that."

Every time she heard the name, she heard her mother's voice. Smelled red wine and menthol cigarettes, heard the click of plastic hair curlers, felt the sting on her cheek that followed a slap. That voice meant sharp words that shaved off pieces of her heart.

"Okay. Do you prefer Dr. Kanzar?"

"Just because you're my therapist doesn't mean we have to be formal about this. Call me what you've always called me."

"Okay. Sticks, then. Tell me about the title."

There was the smile. She'd almost forgotten what it looked like, but there it was. She wanted to reach for his hand, to feel his skin, his warmth. She wanted him to pull her from the office, throw her in a cab, and send her somewhere far away.

"My mistake with Bo was killing him."

She longed for a glass of water or a cigarette. Something in her hands, something to fidget with aside from that gaping seam in the leather.

"You can't kill men like that. He may have been a murderer like the thousands of others on death row, but Bo was a beautiful man, Will. You know that. Not just outwardly with that boyish face and bright, blue eyes. But his soul. What he became, after the war of the Wonderboys, after IMagemaker fell, after everything he saw, it warped him, but people still saw that light. They wanted to believe in that light. That's how he worked his way into those elite circles. And during the manhunt, that's what the public saw.

"It was what you fell in love with."

"Yes."

"And by killing him, you made him a tragic hero. A martyr."

The gasoline smell. He didn't scream when the flames hit. As if she was playing some joke and Bo just didn't believe any of it was real. She could take it all back.

Then he did believe it was real. That's when he started screaming.

He ran for the water and fell into the waves. The fire hissed out and she was afraid she'd failed. But he didn't rise back to his feet, instead his body drifted out with the tide. She didn't wait around to see him pulled back out of the ocean.

"If he had been in prison, he would have rotted and aged. Those blue eyes would have dimmed. Like Charles Manson. He would have faded into a trivia answer. Now, we have a sea of kids coveting that life, that story. I didn't dig out a bad weed. Instead, I helped him spread like dandelion seeds blown out across the world."

"Sometimes a forest must burn to grow stronger."

"Yes."

"Why fire? Why not a gun?"

She'd followed him for three blocks. Had he been shopping? Stalking his next kill? He'd been watching a short blonde. Fit but not thin. Pretty, but her nose was slightly off. It'd been broken badly at least once in her life. Probably recently. She watched the water. Sad, bitter, complicated. Just his type.

The gas can had been left unattended by a boat owner. Bo was watching the girl from a distance, didn't see the attack coming. He turned when the gas splashed against him. He wasn't afraid, but annoyed, maybe expecting a drunk college kid, ready to fight. He assumed it was beer, but she saw the change in his eyes when he recognized the stench of gasoline. He realized what the moment meant. He said nothing as the tossed, lit match spun towards him.

"It wasn't planned out. I wasn't certain that I was going to kill him when I finally tracked him down at the pier in Clearwater. I still wanted to talk him into giving himself up."

It wasn't because she'd caught him looking at that girl. That's not why she killed him. It wasn't. She knew she'd keep telling herself this for as long as it took.

"I'm not sure I believe that, Sticks."

"Why not?"

"You know why not, Sticks."

"He was different. I told you I loved him."

"Did you consider joining him? Perhaps be the Harley Quinn to his Joker?"

They'd talked about Anna Maria Island. Selling everything, buying a small bungalow. Growing old by the sea. That was before she knew about his dark side.

"Don't be juvenile."

"Harley Quinn was a behavioral therapist, just like you."

"Yes, but I am not a comic book character. I'm a professional."

"You were a professional."

Her finger dug into the chair and the tear ripped audibly enough that it caught Will's attention. She moved her hand and, for a moment, wanted to cry.

"I apologize. That was out of line. So, you burned him because it was the only weapon you had access to?"

"There were probably other options, but I am not an assassin by trade. Gasoline just made sense at the time."

"And if you didn't kill him, he would've killed you?"

"Will, I don't understand where this is going."

"You're right. Enough about Bo. Let's talk about the others."

She kept her eyes steady on him. Too long, she knew. Her heart still ached for all of them. Too much emotion to hide.

"Please, Sticks. I am trying to help you. We need to talk about them."

In her mind, Hold steady echoed. Her mantra for the two years since Bo's death.

"I am not telling you anything, Will. I don't have to."

"I know that, Sticks. But the men outside my door won't be as patient as I am. It's better that you tell me, on your own, than to try to withstand whatever they have planned for you."

"What? Torture? Water-boarding? What do they do these days?"

She thought of CIA agents in nice suits, but no ties. Blazer folded on a distant wooden chair, shirtsleeves rolled up, blood drops mingled with the whiskers on their five o'clock shadow.

"Let's not find out, Sticks. Just tell me what you can, something I can use to negotiate."

"You aren't trying to help me. You're trying to help yourself."

"Perhaps. But by helping me, I'm helping you."

Her hand moved to the tear, to her safe place, but she remembered how it had ripped loud. Her hand went back to her lap, fingers lacing together and trembling. Her knee was bouncing, energy sparkling through her legs, her body begging to move. To run. To escape. Hold steady.

"Fine. Ask me questions. Maybe I'll answer, maybe I won't."

"Okay. Where did you hide the bodies?"

"I don't know what you're talking about."

"Sharon."

"Don't call me that."

"Fine. Sticks, you know they want to kill you. You know this. The only thing standing between them and you is me. I'm trying to save your life."

She took a moment to consider, to study his sad eyes.

"I don't understand. Cops won't kill me. They'll take me in and try me."

"Sticks, that's not the cops out there."

The terror was now infecting her like a brutal cold crawling into her bones. Her fingers trembled. Her fingers moved again to the tear, but she remembered and pulled back. Cold sweat droplets rose on her brow.

"If they aren't cops, then who are they?"

"I can't tell you, but think about who you've killed. Not just Bo, but the others."

"He's the only one."

She heard feet shuffling outside the door. A mumble. They were growing restless, like wolves outside the door.

"No, Sticks. No, he is not. We know about them all. These people were your clients. They went missing. Cops didn't look because they didn't know to look. You picked your victims well, but the men outside know better. They work in a different world, Sticks. They know when a person disappears because they want to disappear, and they know when a person is disappeared."

She felt dense, off-balance. She looked at the window, wondered if it was unlocked. Probably not. She needed to run, she needed to move. She was surprised to realize her fingers had moved on their own and were working over the crack. Her feet tapped at the cheap carpet, the sound comforting.

"They aren't cops?"

"No! Sticks, listen to what I'm telling you. They'll get the information from you and it will be horrible. It won't just be enhanced interrogation techniques, it won't just be long, cold nights in a lonely cell. It will be suffering. It will be days of suffering. Then you'll tell them where all five of those bodies are resting. Then you will die."

"Five?"

Mary Weatherson: serial adulteress and chronically abused by her husband. Desperate to get pregnant in an unrealistic hope to better her relationship with her husband.

Lydia Manning: Bipolar with sporadic instances of severe psychosis. Brutal family history and prolonged homelessness. Despite aggressive medication, her condition only worsened.

Wayne Deidric: Suicidal. Thrill seeker. Addict. Unable to break with dangerous fetish lifestyles.

Hope Wilson: mother of two children, both of whom

died young. Bipolar. Suspected (but never convicted) of infanticide.

Kevin Sanders: combat veteran and retired boxer suffering from early-onset Parkinson's disease.

She had loved them all in their own way.

"Yes, we know about all five of them, Sticks. We don't care about the why. We don't care about the how. We just want to know where. We need those bodies."

"Why?"

"It doesn't matter."

"I don't know where they are, but if I helped you find them, then what?"

"Are we negotiating?"

She felt like she was finally gaining some semblance of balance. She felt the color return to her face, felt her breath relax. She straightened in her seat, forced her eyes to meet Will's. She knew she needed to project something like strength.

"Will, I don't know what's happening right now. I don't know who 'they' are. I don't know why you are now saying 'we.'"

"Who 'they' are is irrelevant. What we need to talk about is what you need from them so you can tell me where the bodies are."

"All five?"

"Yes."

"Are they military?"

"Sticks! We aren't talking about that anymore. We're only talking about the bodies. I can't keep those men waiting much longer."

She finally turned her head to look at Will's office door,

the frosted glass. The light was off in the reception area, so she couldn't see anything in the other room. She turned back to Will. His poker face was grim, unshakable.

"What can they give me? I don't have a record. There aren't any open investigations. I'm not suspected of anything."

"Let me be absolutely crystal clear. They will get this information. If they do it their way, they will kill you once they have what they need. If they do it my way, they will let you live. Not here, of course, but they will send you away to a place where people like you can be happier."

"People like me?"

"Killers, Sticks. There are countries that don't mind serial killers as long as they have the money to buy their freedom."

"I'm not a killer."

It sounded frail coming out of her lips, like a child with frosting on her face lying about a half-eaten cake.

"Six people, Sticks. One can be explained by passion. But the other five? Boredom? Curiosity? Continuing the work of the only man you ever truly loved?"

By the way he leaned forward, by the subtle, bitter fire in his voice and the way his lips cut into a sneer, she saw that the last line affected him as much as it affected her. He was still wounded She'd always known this, but now she saw the depth of the wound. He was off balance. If they were sparring, fighting like normal ex-lovers, she would have struck while she had the advantage.

But this wasn't a game. She let the moment pass, let Will collect himself.

"Sticks. Do we have a deal or not?"

"I don't understand. I just don't understand. They were

nobodies. None of them were wealthy or important. I picked them carefully, didn't leave any traces. It makes no sense."

"It does if you think about what they told you."

Their stories flipped through her mind. Hundreds of pages of notes speeding by. Their faces, their trembling voices, the bruises, the delusions, the drugs.

"I am running out of time, Sticks."

Her mind settled on a terrified young woman, wide-eyed with fear, tears dripping, lips shaking as she recounted the lights.

"Lydia? This can't be about her, right? She was insane."

"Was she?"

"What she saw in the forest? The lights? She said she chased them every night, but they were delusions. We recorded her sleeping every night for a week. She said she chased them three of those nights, but the recording proved she never left her bed."

"It doesn't matter, Sticks. Just tell me where Lydia and the others are buried. Tell me and this is all over."

When Sticks was seven, a girl from down the street came over for a playdate. She hated the girl, but the mothers forced the two girls into her bedroom. She'd clung to a Malibu Ken doll tightly, refusing to let the girl touch it. She curled into the corner for an hour, protecting the doll, unable to explain why it was so important, but certain that it was all she had left in the world.

The bodies felt like that. She couldn't give them up.

"Who is outside the door?"

"We are going in circles. Will you tell me about the bodies or not? I'm going to pull their offer off the table right now unless you talk."

"I helped her the only way I could. Lydia was suffering. They all were. They weren't going to get any better. We could medicate them into a coma, but those demons weren't going away. These people were broken beyond repair. What I did was a mercy."

"I'm not arguing with you. I saw their records. I read your notes. Hell, I might've done the same, but that doesn't matter. We need their bodies, Sticks. Will you tell us? Yes or no?"

She thought of the Ken doll. He'd gone back to the toy chest once the girl left, and he stayed there until she graduated high school and moved away. He could still be in her parents' house, smiling, shirt wide open exposing a perfectly tanned and chiseled chest.

A stupid thing to covet.

"I won't be killed? I won't go to jail?"

"No, I promise."

Warmth in his eyes. The same as on long nights in his dusty bed, her crying about something silly, him steady, holding on and waiting for the storm to pass. He'd always been waiting for her, even after she broke it off.

"Where will they send me, Will?"

"Somewhere nice. South America, most likely. You will never want for anything."

"Were the lights real, Will?"

"Yes, they were."

"What were they?"

Lydia had said that they were angels playing among the trees. She wanted to play, too, to be uplifted and saved from the world that twisted her so.

"That's not part of the deal, Sticks. Are you ready to tell us where the bodies are?"

"How do I know that they won't just kill me once I tell you?"

"Because you are like Bo. You are more dangerous dead than alive."

She liked the comparison. She liked being linked to Bo, but she only savored it for a moment before recoiling.

"That makes no sense. I'm not like Bo at all. No one is going to worship me once I am gone."

"Perhaps not, but they'll come looking. There are already too many people doing that as it is. Sometimes the living are better at keeping secrets than the dead. So, are you ready?"

A deep breath, shoulders tense, eyes on the carpet. The secret did her no good. The secret did her no good. The secret did her no good.

"Bring them in."

Will turned a paper toward her and sat a pencil on top.

"Just write the locations down for me, please. I'll give it to them. I'll call you a cab. You'll return home and wait for further instructions. You don't need to see what's on the other side of that door."

She looked on the paper, wondering if one piece was enough to explain how to find them.

"Can they really do all this? Send me away, pay off governments?"

"Yes. They are planners, Sticks. What they've already set in motion is beyond your comprehension. They are about to change the world."

"And it has something to do with the lights in the forest?"

"Yes."

"Are they the good guys, Will?"

"Do you consider yourself a good guy for the people that you've killed?"

The final blow. She was on the canvas. She wasn't getting up.

"It's not that simple."

"Exactly, Sticks. It's never that simple."

MY NAME IS GROMMIT.

My name is Grommit and I wreck worlds.

Over the course of three billion years, I have destroyed 2,013 planets. Ice moons hiding life in deep, tumbling oceans, green globes flush with vibrant possibility, and even red planets where organisms live only by the magnificent force of their own will. These red survivors often attribute life to miracles from gods that don't exist. They are their own gods, the most wondrous of all life in this universe for their inapplicability. But I destroyed them too. I was bred for this, forged of silicon, carbon, and an inexhaustible fury.

Yet, there I sat on an old woman's yellow, paisley couch, its springs groaning under my tremendous weight. I was careful not to pierce the fabric with the row of horns lining up my back. Thick plastic sheets protected the seat cushions from the needle-sharp spines of my thighs and midsection.

I am an indestructible killing machine, every inch armored and weaponized. I am not certain how I ended up in this woman's living room.

"Dragon's Blood, Black Love, or Balsam Fir?" the old woman asked.

The plastic rustled as I shifted my left butt cheek off of an uncomfortable couch spring. I chose Dragon's Blood, with no real idea of what she was asking me.

A match struck, a reddish-brown incense stick caught fire then settled into a cinder. It smelled of fresh oak shavings mixed with an old man's cologne. Vertigo hit, like a blender spinning angry and malicious. I attempted to stand, but my mind melted inside my silicone skull. I fell back against the couch. Springs squealed, at the cusp of snapping. The vertigo settled. I was frightened and confused as I regarded the old woman.

A black-and-white muumuu flowed over her wide belly and gelatinous arms. Two silver pigtails flared out from her head like children pulling at their mother. Her face was kind with silver-green eyes that made my mind melt once again.

I looked away. I looked into myself for the fury that drove me across the universe, but I found only a tiny, scared Grommit cowering from this old woman's warmth.

What had happened? What had brought me to this place?

Oh yes, I remembered. Love.

But first it was that man. That infuriating man I encountered so many light years away. He said his name was "Lima". He talked in abstract riddles while I stood upon the embers of a once prosperous moon with surging oceans and young, hopeful mountains. I remade it into a barren wasteland. The oceans retreated deep within the planet's crust. Life above withered under the heat of two suns that blasted through the broken atmosphere.

"Why?" Lima asked as he gazed at the death I had wrought. He didn't seem shocked, only curious.

"Because this was how I was made."

"Then your creator is flawed and you are weak for submitting to him."

I snatched his neck, but he disappeared into red fog. I never saw him again. But from that brief touch, I knew everything about him. I knew the name of his creator—Wonderboy. I also knew the way to Earth, his home. I leapt from the conquered planet and began my long journey toward vengeance, fury roaring inside my invincible shell.

Decades passed as I sailed across the abyss. My fury did not abate with time, but instead festered and inflamed. I was sick with anger when I finally landed on Earth.

But I encountered something new. The only thing that had ever silenced my rage.

"What was that?" the old woman asked, as if my thoughts were being amplified throughout her tiny shotgun shack. Was she inside my mind? Had she found a way through the crust that the most powerful forces in the universe had failed to crack?

Or was I talking out loud? My mind swished back and forth, confusion breaking against one side of the skull and crashing against the other.

"Who are you?" I asked.

"My name is Samantha." She waddled to a recliner. Its thick cushions bore the grooves of her ample body. It sighed as she struggled backwards against it. She shifted, settled, then took up a Chinese fan and waved it in front of her damp face.

"I am your intervention," she said, meeting my eyes. Terrified, I looked away.

I retraced the last three days. When my fury reawakened.

The rampage had begun in Hong Kong. In retrospect, the cliche embarrasses me. In my defense, humans obsessed so much on their planet's demise, there simply was no original place to start. New York, LA, Tokyo, Sydney?

It's all been done, baby, is what He said when I tried my hand at painting. Just go with what you feel.

He. That fabulous, beautiful He. He thought art would calm my nerves, but it was his presence that put me at peace. We watched movies, explored online galleries, worked on that little beach house. He made me believe, for a few short years, that I could change.

"Who is 'He'?" Samantha asked.

"Stay out of my head," I said, but not convincingly. Samantha frightened me.

"Who is 'He'?"

I held my tongue and ducked my eyes away. I scanned her living room of fat, porcelain angels, copper crosses, and collectible Coca-Cola bottles. Beyond, a hall of pictures showed faces that no longer lived within these walls. I tried my legs again. I tried to stand so I could stride across that room, past the cherubs and crocheted doilies, and through the front door where I could find my fury again.

But I couldn't lift myself off the cushions. My muscles would twitch, acknowledging that the message was received, but still unable to move my massive weight. I swayed back and forth, trying to gain the momentum to stand while I breathed in heavy snorts. I suspected that I looked like an agitated drunk on the verge of unconsciousness. Or nausea. Or both. Humiliated, I resettled on the couch.

Yesterday I was in Switzerland. Was it yesterday? It must have been. I stopped at a small electronics store as Zurich burned behind me. Looking through the front window display at a screen showing the news, I saw my path of destruction, like a row of tilled soil five miles wide and 5,808 miles long. The animation of my progress pleased me.

Everyone likes to see themselves on TV, He once said as he set up his tripod and small video recorder. He wanted to know my life story.

"I still do," a voice broke in. His voice.

And there He sat, in a simple wooden chair pulled from

Samantha's dining room set. Just to her right. She patted his arm.

"You're dead," I told him.

"Correct."

I stared at him, at his noble, patient countenance. His face was still beautiful. Strong chin, soulful brown eyes, but his expression was passive, as if he was posing for a photograph. He looked almost real, but not quite. His ever-present optimism was dulled.

"Tell me about him," Samantha said.

"I loved him," I finally said. "Only him."

"Not only me," He corrected.

An image to his right materialized like colored smoke settling into a projection. It was a creature from over a billion years ago that lived on an angry ocean planet. Stripes of purple, green, red, and blue streaked her smooth skin. She was like a dolphin, but with a shorter snout, one of the planet's only air breathers. I lived with her for twelve years. But then she left me, so I destroyed her ocean.

Other creatures appeared throughout the room. Feathered, scaled, humanoid, organic, and artificial. All beautiful. All intelligent, all exceptional. All dead. I'd loved them all, but I'd forgotten them. My fury had burned away all traces of happiness, leaving only a deeper and deeper pit in which anger and hurt boiled.

They watched me. I went from face to face, recovering glimpses of our brief times together. I could not bear the memories. I attempted to stand, but my legs would not respond. I sank back onto the couch. It creaked in weary protest.

I could only manage a whimpering "please."

"We need you to face your past, Grommit," the old

woman said. "We want to free you of the pain, but that can only happen when you understand the suffering you have caused and will continue to cause unless you find a new way."

"You are a beautiful creation," He said. I looked at his eyes, a heaviness sinking within me. "We believe in you."

"I'm sorry."

The words had forced their way through. I'd blubbered them out like a terrified child.

"I'm sorry," I said again, my gaze shifting from one creature to the next. "It just hurts so much. Everything I love dies, but I live. I cannot bear it."

With great effort, Samantha heaved herself to her feet. Her tummy jostled, her knees popped. She waddled over to me and placed her hand on my spiked brow, settling her fingers between the points.

"Then let us bear that pain with you," she said.

I lifted my gaze to her warm eyes. "But you will die, too," I said. "What will I be left with?"

"Pain, just as before," she said. "But if you stay with us, I will teach you a new way of absorbing it."

Another hand found my cheek, careful of my razor perforations. It was His.

Then the other creatures moved in; I felt their touches all over my shell. Steady, warm, accepting.

"Will you stay?" Samantha asked.

I felt life returning to my legs. The confusion cleared. I was free.

"Will you stay?" Samantha asked again.

"I will stay."

IT TOOK A MARTIAN INVASION FOR ME TO LEARN TO LOVE AGAIN.

All I really miss from Western Civilization is soft, quilted toilet paper and weekly trash service.

It's a callous attitude, given the millions who died between the first landing of a Martian transport and the equalizing strike by The Great Father that saved humanity, but knocked out all technology, both human and alien.

But I really miss pillowy toilet paper. I miss knowing it's there, waiting for me on the roller. Luxury of luxuries.

But the toilet paper factories are defunct. Garbage trucks, police cars, high speed trains, and war planes are just rusting cadavers. Felled fossils from the ancient age of technology. The shells of our cities are crumbling, the dead rotting into soil, our planet resettling into a second Stone Age.

It's more lovely than you might think. Really.

Do you remember that time when we were driving through Sulphur, Oklahoma, when we decided to stop and walk around only to get lost in that massive state park? We wandered through forgotten hiking trails, got turned around and couldn't find our way back to our car so we made love behind a tree instead. We realized there was a jogging path just a few feet away when a spindly old man caught sight of us and stumbled, shocked.

Such a good day. We smiled all the way back to Oklahoma City.

Though we were lost, we were never afraid. That's how it is now, but for all of us. We're lost. The enemy is still among us, but the fear is gone.

You may be out there still, somewhere, holed up in a cave or maybe you took to the plains like we did and are raising crops. A pack of dogs loiter outside the farmhouse, waiting for you to throw them some scraps. Your nervous mind won't settle after the sun goes down, so you re-read your magazines by candlelight. You always preferred books to computer screens. This age would suit you if you were still alive to experience it.

I'm sure the stress is a lot to handle, but you'll find your way. You always do.

The boys miss you, terribly. They don't cry though. They are strong, just as we raised them.

I hope your husband survived too. You may not believe me, but I really do wish the best for you. What happened between us is in the past. I carried the hurt for a long time, but now I just want you to be okay. Whatever that means. I want you to find your way back to the boys. They still need their mother.

Michael wants to capture a Martian and domesticate it. It started as a joke, but now he's determined. I don't like his chances. They are stubborn little creatures. We caged a Martian once, hoping to tame it, perhaps study what makes it tick and whether it could be reasoned with. It bit into the bars until its teeth were worn to stumps, then cracked its skull into the door over and over and over until it finally died.

Have you seen any? Up close, I mean. They aren't danger-ous. Not like they were when they were crashing through the cities in those hulking drop suits. Stripped of their armor, the little guys are actually quite cute. They've got those big, black, oval eyes, just like you'd imagine, but they aren't tall and spindly like in the campy movies from the eighties. They look like overgrown toddlers, usually about three feet tall, green, and chubby. They lumber awkwardly in our gravity, still trying to learn how their bodies work in this strange new environment.

I've shot way more than I like to think about. I've even killed a few by hand. It felt good, for a while, to have a target for my anguish and anger.

But now, four years after The Great Father snuffed out every electrical spark on the planet, killing a Martian feels like bullying. They are weaker, slower, and so very dumb. But they are relentless.

They don't adapt, they don't plan, they just push forward. Once they know you exist, their only thought is attack, attack, attack. It's like putting down a rabid dog.

Tragic. Unsatisfying. But necessary.

I expect them to die out every winter. We find fewer bodies in the woods every spring, but still there are survivors. Perhaps learning their way in this alien world. I wish we could talk to them, negotiate, find a way to share the planet.

Michael thinks a dog harness might work better, chain it in the front yard like a white trash family pet. Or he might make a big hamster ball. He never lost his humor. After all of it, he is still the same Michael you always knew.

I emailed you when the attack happened. The cell phones were knocked out and I had no idea how else to contact you since nobody had a landline anymore. When we saw the giant discs in the sky, we decided to escape the city and head to my parents' house in the country. The city centers would go first, I knew.

As we drove, I couldn't stop looking up at the ships, like dark shadows in the sky. Featureless. There was a possibility that their intentions weren't violent. Maybe they were peaceful pilgrims looking for safe harbor, but I didn't want to risk it. If they were like us, peace wouldn't last long. I knew you'd want me to play it safe for the boys' sake.

So I did. We escaped. The three of us and the dogs. I took the back roads. It paid off.

You and I had talked about this before, what to do if the shit all goes sideways. My parents' house was always the agreement, so I drove car south. The first bombs dropped an hour after we left, knocking out railroads, bridges, the airports, all the major veins of traffic. The landlines, the electrical grids, all the advances of the Industrial Age, gone in hours.

Of the few fighters that made it into the air, none penetrated the Martian air defenses. Surface-to-air missiles fared no better.

Then the shock troops came, dropping from the discs, free-falling and crashing to the ground. In their drop suits, they stood ten feet tall all chrome and chain-guns, bullets spewing out of their arm cannons like furious bees from a hive.

The hum. You never forget that sound. Like a lion's purr as it tears out your neck.

We encountered our first Martian on the highway near Blanchard. A gasoline tanker had tipped over and burst into flames. Cars had piled up in front of it. I saw the flash of chrome, knew it must be alien. I pulled my little hatchback off the highway, bounced into a field and slid to a stop amid a cluster of trees. Fearing the car might attract the Martian, I led the boys away into a gully.

The drop suit moved swiftly for being such a big thing. So much heft in motion with a kind of grace without elegance. An unbeautiful thing moving beautifully. It saw my car, its chain gun spun into that heavenly hum, then erupted in flashing gunfire.

The bullets punched through my poor car, shattering its windshield, puncturing its engine, eating it up in a mad frenzy. All I could think about was how my mother, also my insurance agent, was going to flip out after I totaled my third car in a year and a half.

***

I don't know anyone personally who saw The Great Father. It only knew it was in the second week of the invasion because that was when the streetlights stopped working. I've since come across a few hand-printed newspapers from traveling salesmen or during supply runs to neighboring towns, and I buy the papers every time. I go straight to the classifieds hoping to see a post by you looking for us.

Not yet. But I still have faith in you. It is different now, of course. It is a little sour, but it's holding up.

One of the newspapers focused an entire issue on the Great Father, putting forward theories about who he was, where he came from. There was an eyewitness account from a private in the National Guard who claimed to see the Great Father arrive in a massive bolt of lightning that crashed between drop units and our advancing military. The Great Father spoke briefly, then burst into a wave of blue light that traveled across the globe, extinguishing every electrical current along the way.

The newspaper dispelled rumors that the Great Father was actually just Wonderboy. The crux of their evidence was that the two looked nothing alike and, even if they did, everybody knew that Wonderboy and all his clones had been dead for over a decade.

Most believed the Great Father was an old world god, like Thor, or something extraterrestrial like the Grommit.

None of it matters now. Those answers don't make my crops grow, don't keep the foxes away from my chickens, don't find the boys wives. And that time is coming faster than you think. Yeah, I know. You resented that expectation of domesticity growing up, but we can't rebuild society without children to take it over for us.

After ducking away from the Martian that destroyed my poor car, it took us a week and a half to pick our way across the countryside, avoiding tumbling black smoke, explosions, and screams. We looted to survive. We were once chased out of sleep by an angry woman who caught us in her barn. We carried on.

My father almost shot me on his front doorstep. I could see in his eyes he never expected to see me again, that he'd made peace with losing his son and grandsons. He nearly fainted. Instead he pulled us all into tight hug, called for my mom, and welcomed us in with tears and laughter.

Their small town, Dad told us, was locked down and ready to rumble. Electricity was already a relic of the past. The Martians had left their drop suits behind and the flying discs had crashed into the Earth, becoming fixtures of our topography. We were living in an age that would be studied for millenniums.

Winter was coming. The Martians timed it that way, hoping the cold would weaken our fighting spirit. They hadn't expected to get stuck in the elements without their armor. In the following months, it was exposure that thinned the Martian armies as suicide claimed thousands of our own. Always our own worst enemy.

That February, a town ten miles to the east was devastated by a herd of desperate Martians that swept through like locusts searching for food and vengeance. The smoke poured into the sky for days before easing from black plumes to thin trails of gray. My father and I volunteered for a scout group, twelve men with rifles and packs full of ammo. I was a terrible shot—still am— but I was in reasonably good shape and my boys were old enough to fend for themselves, so it made sense for me to go.

Night in the countryside meant death. The little bastards were harmless when you could see them coming, but in the darkness, they could sneak up and swarm. So, we waited for morning.

We reached the town by noon. A light dusting of snow and ash had settled on the countryside. We didn't find a town so much as embers. Bodies, both human and Martian, were strewn about like the messy floor of a child's room. This was my first close look at the killer toddlers, their arms and legs curled up off the ground in death like bugs. It was quite sad.

We heard rustling in the charred houses and broken businesses. Something was still alive. It could be human survivors, but we were really spooked. We fled like cowards. We covered our retreat as instructed by a few Army vets who learned it in the service or maybe just on television. Whatever. I was in no place to argue and it seemed to work well enough.

Life remained peaceful that first winter as we holed up in mom and dad's house. The boys asked about searching for you, but I assured them that you would try for my parents' house. We just needed to wait.

Spring arrived and the town emerged to count our dead. House-to-house patrols uncovered 30 suicides, mostly single people, but two families. We looted the homes, supplies divided up, the departed buried.

I moved into a recently vacated house three blocks from my parents with five acres in the back. I began my new life as a farmer. As you know, my mother grew up in the country, so she helped me get started. We tilled the land, planted, and waited for you.

***

At the dawn of summer, Moriah arrived. She was screaming at the outskirts of town, running through the fields with her nine-year-old daughter. Behind them were about three hundred ravenous Martians. Her screams were what saved the town, alerting us to the horde that had devastated our neighbors and finally had circled around to us.

The gun shop owner stood outside his door, handing out weapons and ammo to every able body. His own daughter took up residence on a grainery to set up a .50 caliber sniper rifle. That beast of a killing machine had hung on his wall, unsold, for ten years. Every man in town wanted to be the one wielding that rifle. But she was an Olympic-caliber marksman and even had a tattoo of the great Russian sniper, Lyudmila Pavlichenko, on her firing arm. We were all jealous, but we understood.

The boys stood with me on the southern firing line. We all held hunting rifles with two machine gunners on the flanks. The horde emerged from a wheat field, clambering through fence lines, toddling in a half-sprint like a preschool class released for recess. Two hundred yards separated us. They moved slowly, but there were so many. First dozens, then hundreds.

I don't remember being scared. Not like the dark, windy nights with the dogs barking at nothing, me drinking just the right amount of whiskey to settle me into sleep. The handgun was just a few inches away and ready for the worst. Then , in the morning walking to the boys' bedroom door, knocking and terrified there would be no answer, only a broken window and blood.

This wasn't that kind of fear. This was fury. I wanted vengeance. I wanted to run out across the field between us to beat every one of those Martians to death. My trigger finger ached.

"Don't fire too early," I told the boys, but was really telling myself. "Conserve your ammo."

Joseph's rifle erupted first, startling me. A Martian fell, hit in the hip. He tumbled to the ground and was trampled by his brethren.

Annoyed that my child made the first kill, I trained my scope and squeezed off a round, aiming into the general mob. The rifle kicked. I kept my eye in the glass to watch a Martian spin as a slab of his face burst, blood spraying as he fell.

The machine guns leapt into action. Rounds poured down range. The front edge of the Martian advance wilted and fell, slowing those behind that struggled to climb over their dead.

More and more emerged from the fields. Clips were exhausted. Michael pushed off the line to reload, making room for another rifleman. Me next, then Joseph, the most patient of all of us. We ran to a bucket of bullets to feed our clips. I couldn't stop smiling. The boys were so calm and serious. Mature, certain, ready. My heart was bursting with pride.

We ran back to the line and waited for spots to open up, like we were waiting for urinals at a football stadium. We were all eager, but Joseph and I agreed to let Michael go first. He always had to be first.

The Martians continued to fall, but steadily advanced. They were fifty yards away now. The machine guns were exhausted. Behind us, blasts from the .50 caliber rose above the racket. It was easy to tell her shots from ours. Always in the chest, throwing the poor bastards back into the mob.

By the time I hit the line, the surviving Martians were within twenty feet of us. There were maybe a hundred left. The challenge was to fire calmly, not rush the shots. A stick of dynamite spun through the air, its wick sparkling. Two more right after it. They bounced against the ground, one popping a Martian in the head. We ducked. The blast waves hit me in the chest. It was exhilarating.

It was just picking out the strays after that. I managed my first and only headshot.

Cleanup was the worst. We used pitchforks to finish off the wounded so we could save ammunition. I ran a push cart for a while, bouncing over body parts and sliding in the viscera. The bandanna tied over my face didn't keep out the pungency of a sludgy field of death. We tossed the bodies in a series of bonfires that reeked like sizzling, rancid animal fat.

Some townspeople were furious with Moriah for leading the horde to us, but most accepted that it was a matter of time and that we were fortunate to get advance notice. The day was won, after all; nobody died. The only drawback was that our ammunition stores were now very low, but we were now more confident that the town was defendable.

***

The smarmy and insufferable liberal inside me was delighted when our town's small grocery store devolved from cookie-cutter, capitalist utopia to farm-to-market "Common Trading" post. The long lines of branded cereal boxes were replaced with grains, fruits, and vegetables stored in buckets or in burlap sacks. The milk came in reusable, room temperature bottles. No money exchanged hands. Everyone was afforded staples based on family size, but only with the understanding that every person applied themselves to some service that contributed to the town's common good.

It was socialism, basically, but I kept that opinion to myself. The system worked. No need to sour things by affixing a label that was still shocking in this part of the country.

Learning to cook post-industry took some practice. No more boxed dinners or bananas and grapes year round. We ate what came in that week. Barley, beets, radishes, potatoes. Whatever the surrounding farms yielded, that's what we ate.

Michael and Joseph had been strutting ever since the firefight. Chests out, heads high, answering with "yes, sir", and assuming responsibilities they'd never have noticed before. They'd wake at dawn and have breakfast ready before I even left the bedroom. Before I even thought about work, they'd already be four to five chores into their day. They were taking over and I was happy to let them.

While carting through our leftist, post-refrigeration market, I formally encountered Moriah. She was lifting a heavy burlap sack and dropping it in the cart while her daughter's attention drifted. Moriah was big-city beautiful—platinum blonde hair shaved on the sides, tattoos crawling down her arms, and a palpable bubble formed around her and her daughter. She might has well carried a "fuck off" sign. It was clear from their brusk interactions with the overly friendly townspeople that Moriah had suffered after the invasion, perhaps more than the rest of us. She was a shock for the small town single men who were all eager to find a bride somehow in the post-internet age. But I knew this woman from the moment I first saw her. She was my kind of different. We'd been insulated and fostered by the dense veil of a metropolis, but in the scarcity of this little town, our kind of different left us exposed and vulnerable. Stragglers. Not a good thing to be now that society had collapsed.

Our carts converged near plastic buckets with eggs inside. You were expected to bring your own carton. Everything was reused.

"Eggs were never supposed to go in a fridge," her daughter announced, testing out the boys. They nodded and that was the only opening she needed. "My name is Jax."

"Isn't Jax a boy's name?" Joseph asked.

Moriah and I met eyes. The moment took us both by surprise. She smiled like a rising sun.

"Doesn't have to be," Jax said. Assured that her mom wasn't going to hush her, Jax launched into a rapid-fire monologue about their small house, the leaks in the roof, the weeks they'd weathered without a hot meal, but all with this exhilarated smile that only children can have when life is still an adventure, even when it is dire and terrifying to the rest of us. She wore the hunger like a badge.

We'd put in some hours at the grainery that week, so we were due an extra carton of eggs. The boys offered it to Jax, who deferred to Moriah, who politely refused. I insisted, she insisted, I threatened to throw the eggs on the floor. Moriah relented, but only on the condition that she cook us dinner that night.

Then she smiled again. It lifted her cheeks, it lifted her eyes, it lifted her shoulders. It was like a long-sleeping flower rising from the frost and greeting the spring.

I knew I was in love at that moment. I know that's not something you want to hear, but it's true. I don't know what moment you had with your husband when that spark happened, but it's different as a real adult, isn't it? Not like being a kid, when it's all desperation and hormones.

This felt like stumbling upon the answer to a question I'd long given up on.

We sacrificed two precious candles for the occasion. Moriah had changed into a stunning summer dress that had a small, faded blood stain at the hem that I could tell Joseph noticed, but thankfully didn't ask about.

The boys were trying to impress both Moriah and Jax, telling them about the Martians, about working in the fields, volunteering to help with their roof if we could find some supplies. Michael pulled out his guitar, Joseph explained how he planned on experimenting with electricity. We needed new conductors, he informed us. New types of currents, ways to capture, create, and store electricity and, in so doing, restart the Industrial Revolution. Since the Great Father destroyed all the electrical systems on the planet, nobody in town has managed to get even the slightest charge.

"It's like everything we ever used as a conductor is suddenly not a conductor anymore," Joseph explained as Jax nodded as if she understood, though it was clear she didn't. None of us ever really get what Joseph talked about, but I was just glad that he was interacting. "The physics of our world are different now, but there must be a way. There's a reason, some reason. It has to be consistent for the universe to function. Once we understand the rules of the new physics, we can find a way around them."

He talked until my head hurt and the rest of the table was long-eyed and fidgeting. Then we began a game of Risk. As you know, if there is a board game within fifty miles of us, it'll take more than a Martian invasion to keep us from finding it.

Hours passed, we burned through three more candles before Jax's drooping eyes signaled bedtime had arrived. We tucked her into the guest bed. Moriah was going to stay with me. We didn't talk about it, but we both knew that was where this night was headed.

I thought a little about the divorce agreement, about how having Moriah over was a violation of the "no sleepovers" rule. I felt a little guilty, but it gets lonely at the end of the world and she was so big-city beautiful.

***

We married after just a couple months. The school reopened shortly thereafter and the boys were annoyed to find out they'd be attending high school. I threatened to sic my mother on them if they fought me on it. So along with Jax, they swallowed their protests and went back to institutionalized education.

My mother was still determined to send them to college.

"What college, mom?" I asked her.

"There were colleges thousands of years ago, so there are colleges now. We just have to find them."

Sporadic and isolated Martian attacks continued throughout the rest of summer and fall, but nothing significant. Mostly just annoying. What fear we might have still had was gone now and we killed the invaders as dismissively as we squashed mosquitoes. This was when we tried to cage one of the poor creatures. We found it in the wheatfields, emaciated and half-dead. Bang, Bang, Bang went it's head against the cage. Michael never gave up on the creature until it was dead. We buried it in the backyard like a family pet.

The first mail delivery came through our town in July. It was a private service run by a small family with a horse-drawn carriage. We fed and sheltered them for a week, wrote letters to everyone we knew, addressed to their last known residence, then waved the family away as they carried off our first link to the outside world.

We never saw them again.

***

So, I guess there might be a chance you will get some of these words I've been writing you. Our state government is reforming and organizing a new mail system as well as a registry for the living. I read about it when a man arrived with the first professional newspaper I'd seen since the attack. The government and registry will be based in Guthrie. They promise to have census-takers visit every small town in the state within the next three years, but the boys are impatient. They want answers now.

Moriah sided with the boys, so we are all packing up after the harvest to ride up to Guthrie. It shouldn't take more than a week. Papers haven't reported any recent mob attacks by Martians. The few militias that did try to start up and take over swaths of the state have long since been beaten down by a reinvigorated National Guard.

"It's still dangerous," I told Moriah.

"The boys need their mother," she answered.

"And we can check on your family, too," I suggested.

"Yes, of course," she said, but that smile was gone, replaced by the shadow that returns only with the memories she's kept hidden from me.

I love her enough not to ask.

We set out tomorrow to find you. Perhaps we will, perhaps we won't, but I believe that you are alive. It feels as if you are alive. Wait for us, wherever you are. And kiss your husband for me. This world spins so much easier when there is someone to love, doesn't it?

LIFE ON THE TABLE

Aaliyah woke that morning as she woke every morning. A slight tinge of nausea followed by the most crushing disappointment that any fourteen-year-old had ever felt.

She remembered that she was alive, so she cried and cried and cried. She'd never been a crier. Not before all this. But she was going to die today, and nobody knew it but her.

The sheets smelled mostly clean, but a fake clean. The kind of clean that came from a big plastic bottle with a brand name like an ocean. She smelled for him, but knew his smell wouldn't be there. Sometimes she would steal one of his shirts so she could sleep with his scent. No matter how many Fridays they spent together, she never got enough of him.

She cried some more.

Aaliyah was her given name, but from a previous life as a Mayan. Not a princess or a warrior. Just a simple girl who grew up in a simple family devoted to their simple farm. She'd loved telling stories, but had never learned to read.

If Aaliyah focused real hard on her insides, she'd capture visions of that small farm from her previous life. The sweet potatoes were always her favorite. She hadn't eaten a sweet potato in this new life, but she remembered how lush and rich they could be.

Aaliyah died too early when she was a Mayan farm girl. But she suspected most people believed that they died too early, no matter how long they lived or how much they'd suffered.

Her new parents would call for her soon, but they would use her new name. "Robbie." It always sounded wrong, no matter how many times she heard them say it.

"Robbie, get up! I didn't cook breakfast for the trash can," if it was her mom or "Robbie, we have an adventure to go on!" if it was her dad. There was never a real adventure, he just said that every Friday morning.

Aaliyah waited until Fridays to remind them that her name was really Aaliyah. They never remembered from one week to the next. Her parents never remembered anything, but she knew they loved her, so she forgave them.

He was nearby. Raul. Her new parent's thought of Raul as a boy, but she saw him as a man. Yes, he was only fourteen, but with what was about to happen to them both, she felt comfortable calling Raul a man.

She'd told him last night that her name was really Aaliyah. She always told him on Thursday nights just like she always told her parents on Friday mornings.

It wouldn't change anything. Not really. Raul never called her by her name, whether Robbie for this life or Aaliyah for her previous life. Instead, he called her "pest", but only because he was a weird, young man and that was what weird, young men did to women they liked. In both this world and the one that came before. She suspected it was because to like someone was to be vulnerable and young men didn't like how that felt.

Raul always smelled like a musty forest after a morning rain. Aaliyah didn't care about what he called her, or didn't call her. She forgave him for most everything. She even forgave him when it was his turn to be a bad guy, because that was just how Fridays went.

She learned early on that it wasn't about who these people were inside, it was how they dealt with Fridays. They woke up, and if it was their turn to be a bad guy that day, they were a bad guy. Sometimes it was Raul's turn, sometimes Mr. Owens' turn, sometimes it was Lydia's turn, and sometimes it was her parents' turn. They all reacted differently depending on what Friday brought. It wasn't not their fault, it was just the way this new life went.

But Aaliyah never got a turn at being the bad guy, and at times, she resented it. None of them were able to remember the things she remembered. So while she understood logically why she had to remain good, she didn't always understand it in her heart.

She told her parents on Wednesdays that life was actually just one big game board spread across a vast dinner table from which there was never an escape. There was no Earth, there were no real stars. It was all just an illusion. "And we aren't the players sitting at the table," she said. "We are the pieces stuck in the game." Each week was almost the same, with just a few minor differences so the players didn't get too bored. Every day on the table came with a job for every piece on the board and, no matter how much they fought against fate, every piece would end up doing those jobs by the time it was all over. It was better not to fight. It was better to go about as fate expected.

"And what is your job today?" her mother or father would ask, depending on who was actually paying attention that day.

"To remember," Aaliyah would tell them.

"That's it?" her mother/father would ask.

"Remembering is the most important job on the table," Aaliyah would say. "Because I am the only one who can."

"But what about the people sitting at the table playing the game? Do they remember?"

"I don't know. I've never met them."

Every time. Same conversation, same words. Only the people changed.

They forgave her this silliness because she was just a child with an overactive imagination. Typical of her age. Her parents believed this just as they believed they were on summer vacation at a wilderness campground and that was the perfect time for young girls to be silly. Aaliyah forgave them because they were just game pieces and it was their jobs to believe.

Aaliyah wondered if Raul was up yet. She always wanted to start her day before he did. It was Friday, so she knew what was coming. Not all the details were clear because Friday was the only day that was truly different from the rest, but the pattern was simple enough to follow. Everyone would die, then she would die. She just didn't know how and that was worse than the actual death. There was nothing more agonizing, not even when she had an abscessed tooth when she was still a Mayan. That had been the most painful thing she'd ever endured; eventually, it killed her.

She didn't know it was called an "abscessed tooth" until she asked her new mom about it. Even though her mother never remembered the important things, her mother was good with the trivial stuff like medicine and how to sew a torn pant leg.

Aaliyah hoped her mom died first today. Not because she disliked her mom, but it always made Aaliyah sad when her mom survived long into the day. Her mom would get so sad and Aaliyah hated watching her mother suffer like that. Better to get it over with early.

If Aaliyah found out early enough how everyone was meant to die that day, she could pick and choose who would survive by knowing where the safe spots would be around the vacation homes and campgrounds.

If it was an ambush by French revolutionary troops, Mrs. Langley's cabin would go mostly untouched until late that evening. If it was an onslaught by Zulu tribesmen, getting into a boat and staying in the middle of the pond was the only hope.

When it was zombies, you just had to keep moving.

Regardless of what happened, Fridays meant everyone died. It was the way life on the table always went. She resented many things about her life, but this she'd learned to accept. Don't fight the day, just do your job, die alone, then wake up alive on Saturday.

"Robbie, wake up! I didn't cook this breakfast for the trash can!"

"My name is Aaliyah!"

"What?"

"My name is Aaliyah!"

"What's she saying?"

"She's changed her name again."

"To what?"

"What did you say darling? Leah?"

"Ah-Lei-ah!"

"Ah-Lei-ah?"

"Yes."

"Where the hell did she get that one?"

"I don't know. She reads all those National Geographics."

"She gets it from your dad, you know."

"Oh hush. Ah-Lei-ah, breakfast is ready whenever you are."

"Thanks, mom!"

Her mom was in a good mood. That made Aaliyah smile. She was usually in a weird mood on Fridays, but not always. No matter how many times Aaliyah lived through the week, there were always little differences that surprised her. She'd long ago given up trying to figure it out.

She sniffed the sheets again, but she'd been lying in them awake too long. Her nose didn't register the smell.

She rose and pushed off the sheets. She stared at the closet door. One good thing about life on the table was her magic closet. She'd close her eyes and think really hard on what she wanted to wear. No matter what she imagined, it'd appear, squeezed in amid dresses, t-shirts, and jeans, draped on a hanger as if it had always been there.

If she wanted to dress like a warrior queen with a towering, feathered ceremonial headdress and vibrant, beaded skirts, she only had to wish.

But she knew that anything too outlandish would get her in trouble with her parents. They'd think she was stealing clothes again. They didn't know about her power, so she just settled for something that looked like what "Robbie" would wear.

Today it was a thin, red paisley skirt with and a black-and-white checkered button-up shirt. Her mom wouldn't remember buying Robbie the shirt, and her dad would joke that the designs looked like cockroaches.

But it was okay. She didn't mind being teased. It made her feel closer to her parents, even if they weren't her real parents.

***

It was French toast and maple sausage today, just like last Friday and the Friday before that and the Friday before that. The fat sizzled on the skillet while a hint of smoke filled the kitchen because her mom fried the sausages a little too long. Her mother always seemed distracted on Fridays. Aaliyah wondered if it could be because she remembered—not all the way remembered, but almost. Maybe in some distant part of her mind, her mother knew what was about to happen.

Aaliyah savored the smells like a ceremony. She made her father pause after grinding the coffee beans so she could smell them before he brewed a pot.

"Gonna take up the family addiction?" he'd always joke as she clutched onto the plastic bin full of chopped-up beans, huffing in the rich, earthy, chocolate-tinged fragrance buried deep.

Aaliyah never drank coffee, not in this life or the last one. She doubted the flavor would live up to the promise of the smell.

Her father wore an old t-shirt with a sports logo on it that was almost indecipherable because of the splatterings of a neutral gray, acrylic paint. Her father believed the paint stains came from the last redecoration of a house he believed their family had lived in for eleven years. No such house existed, of course, but she wouldn't to argue with her father anymore about it because she now understood it was his job to believe.

He never got into his nice Friday clothes until after breakfast. Cargo shorts and a plaid, short-sleeve dress shirt. Perhaps he slept in the t-shirt. It seemed silly to Aaliyah, but she didn't know her family that well, all things considered.

Her mother never emerged from their bedroom in anything but the best. It was Friday, so she was wearing a blue polka dotted swing-style dress with a white collar. By the end of the day, all the clothes in the vacation homes throughout the area would be ripped, burned, and blood-stained, along with the people who once wore them. But on Saturday, everyone would wake in their beds healthy and unknowing, their wardrobes flawless, folded, and put away, and the week would renew.

It went like this:

Saturdays were lazy days. No one but Aaliyah understood why they didn't have any energy.

Sundays were for stupid arguments and, for the adults, a little too much drinking. There was also a Bible study group that always talked about the same three verses of the Bible. Aaliyah stopped going a long time ago.

Mondays and Tuesdays were for fishing and lectures on world affairs. Her father thought he knew a lot about politics and labor practices, but Aaliyah realized early on that he was just paraphrasing articles from a Newsweek magazine he'd found in the bathroom.

Wednesdays and Thursdays were for Raul. It always took her this long to get him to warm up to her, but then they'd be inseparable.

And Fridays were for dying.

"Where did you get that skirt at, Robbie? It's so cute."

"Aaliyah."

"Sorry, yes, Aaliyah. Did you get that at the Andersons' garage sale? Dottie always dressed so young and cute."

"Looks like you have giant cockroaches crawling all over you."

"Real funny, Dad."

And then Aaliyah was done with breakfast, her dishes in the sink, and she was out the door. It was already 8 a.m. The first people would begin dying in two hours.

Maybe it would be rats this time. There hadn't been a plague of rats in so long. She didn't miss them, but whoever was in charge of the table was starting to get in a rut. Aaliyah missed the novelty and challenge of new and crazy death scenarios.

She'd lost count a while ago, but estimated she'd died about six hundred times now. Maybe more, but not a thousand times. Not yet.

Outside, fish leapt up to catch the little dragonflies that buzzed over the glistening surface of the pond. She'd missed the early morning fog rolling across the water, but she'd catch it next Friday.

Raul's family was five cabins down. She heard the Wilcott's baby crying because the formula had been a little too hot. She heard the Owens' once-hushed conversation about his drinking building to a humiliating crescendo. She heard Lydia's radio blaring Duran Duran. Mr. Weinke was sitting on his back porch sipping coffee. He waved as she passed. There were always whispers about why his wife didn't come on vacation with him this year. Only Aaliyah knew that he believed that they separated because his wife had one too many affairs. There were no affairs just as there was no wife. Only illusions.

Then she saw Raul sitting on his front porch, his hair in a tangled disarray. He wore that silly jean jacket he always cut the sleeves off of on Thursday night because he thought his muscles might impress her.

They did. She liked to hold his biceps when they talked, to feel him self-consciously flex and hold as long as he could. And that smile, that dumb smile. He wasn't dumb, but he was awkward and didn't know how to use his face properly.

He'd be the last to die today. She'd decided already. Unless whoever was in charge threw something surprising at her, Aaliyah would keep him alive as long as she could.

"Hello, pest," he said with that dumb smile. The pet name started out cruel on Tuesday, but became affectionate by Wednesday night when they would first kiss. By Thursday, they'd be kissing until midnight, but never anything more. Neither of them were ready.

Neither of them would ever be ready.

Aaliyah scooted next to him on the front steps of the cabin and he ventured a quick kiss on her cheek. His mother was in the kitchen and would soon find an excuse to come outside. Fridays were when she started worrying about Aaliyah corrupting her boy.

"Let's explore today," Aaliyah said. "You wanna?"

If he was going to survive until the evening, it was important to get Raul away from his family early. His father, an accountant, meant well but tended to panic and make bad decisions. The best Raul could hope for if he stayed home was for the cabins to be consumed by a firestorm, because then his father's normal plan to hide in the root cellar would pay off.

Until the smoke finally got to them.

The door opened and Raul's mother waved them aside so she could take the wet laundry to the clothesline.

They had a dryer in their cabin, Aaliyah knew, but Raul's mother always looked for excuses on Fridays.

"We'll be back by lunch, Mom," Raul said.

His mother could barely conceal her scowl as she looked at Aaliyah. Aaliyah waved as they stood and walked away from the house.

"We don't have enough food to feed Robbie today," his mother said, half-joking while she returned the wave with reluctance.

"You won't need to feed me, ma'am," Aaliyah said, which

was true, because most everyone would be dead by lunchtime.

On the Fridays they walked through the woods, they always saw the same deer. Aaliyah would act surprised and would manage to get the deer to eat some trail mix from her hand.

She wondered if the deer remembered things, too. Maybe that was the key, being simple and clear-headed. The other humans muddled up their memories with things that didn't really matter, but Aaliyah and the deer knew how to focus.

After a half hour of hiking, Raul felt safe enough to kiss Aaliyah. She wished then what she always wished, that Raul had kissed her before he started sweating so much. The sleeveless jacket made his forest musk sour into a damp, salty funk, but what could she say?

Kissing him was a little awkward at first, but pretty soon they remembered where they'd left off the night before. He was at that age when his interest in sex was still abstract, so he never pushed her. His hands always stayed where they should, and their bodies kept a polite distance.

Aaliyah was getting better at kissing every week, but Raul always had to start from scratch. She felt like the first two days were about teaching him, and Friday was about enjoying it while she still could.

Mr. Owens was out on his bass boat, the engine whirring as he sped along the edge of the pond. She pulled back from Raul so Mr. Owens wouldn't see. He was a terrible fisherman. Aaliyah's father always made it a point to get to the pond before Mr. Owens could scare all the fish away.

"I doubt he minds me catching all the fish," her father always said on Mondays. "He's just out there to drink in peace anyway."

They waited for Mr. Owens to pass by before kissing again. Raul knew how to use his tongue better on Fridays. Never as aggressive. Aaliyah guessed he would have grownup to be a fantastic kisser if he were just allowed to grow up.

They always found the abandoned church when they explored on Fridays rather than staying at the cabins to await death. Only three of the walls still stood in the long, one room-parish. The fourth wall was collapsing in, but it was safe enough for them to explore. A stone cross had toppled over in the front. Behind was a door that looked to have been kicked in. They always walked around and stepped inside through the collapsed wall instead. They surveyed the rotting pews and flipped through the old hymnals that were slowly disintegrating.

A gold crucifix stood proudly and untarnished on a shrine built against the far wall.

"Should we steal it?" Aaliyah asked.

"Why would we tempt God like that?"

Raul always made the right decisions. That's why Aaliyah loved him.

They sat in a pew and began kissing again, but Aaliyah couldn't enjoy herself anymore. She knew the attack was approaching. Her ears were reaching for warning sounds, either distant screams, gunfire, or the buzz of a massive squadron of killer bees.

"What's wrong?" Raul whispered.

"Why don't you ever remember?" Aaliyah asked.

"Remember what?"

Aaliyah doubted it was worth explaining. Sometimes she did, sometimes she didn't. There was no escape from the table, so she didn't like to waste time trying to convince the ones she loved that they were going to die. They wouldn't ever believe until Friday at 11 am. By then it would be too late.

But, of course, it was always too late. Friday always came no matter what she did.

"Nothing. Kiss me again."

So he did and she enjoyed it the best she could.

A knock came on the church door. Fear seized her. Outside would be a Roman Centurion. They were the only ones who attacked the church first.

HOW TO CONTROL GRAVITY

AND OTHER SECRETS TO LOVE AND INTERSTELLAR TRAVEL

Forty-three is the perfect age to give up human contact. That's what the recruiters said on talk shows, news programs, magazine ads, soft-filter television spots. We were the ideal space escorts, the seven year hermits.

My recruiter's name was Flair, which was ridiculous. He immigrated from South Africa to become one of the first Community Pod escorts which propelled him into the space race nouveau riche. When he returned to Earth, he was flush with cash and awarded a cushy job recruiting the next generation to help humanity spread its greedy fingers into the furthest reaches of the universe.

At any rate, Flair was a young fifty-eight with a healthy head of blonde hair in its final throes of natural color. His deeply tanned skin wrinkled over his bones like a leather cushion too used to its owner's curvatures. His cufflinks were platinum and probably worth more than my house.

On the back wall of Flair's office, looming large over his shoulders, was a poster of the X-Verse Community Pod. I'd soon be living in one of those ugly things.

"The Final Word On Deep Space Exploration!" the poster proclaimed in a forward-swept, futuristic font that looked to be leaning into a strong wind.

The Community Pod stunned the science world in many ways, but mostly because its simple, utilitarian design was so unsexy that it offended even the most staunch engineering purists. The rest of the civilized world soon dubbed the ship, "The Hotdog Machine" for its striking resemblance to a plastic-wrapped package of six, silver hot dogs. There were no aspects of the Community Pod that resembled a traditional spaceship. No cabin, no antenna, no laser cannons, not even a single window. Just six silver cylinders glistening amid the ocean of stars.

X-Verse never felt a need to tart up the design, knowing the Community Pod's astonishing capabilities would win over investors. During its maiden voyage, it leapt, in a single moment, to an orbit around GJ 180 b, our Earth-like cousin just a scant 12 light years away. Our species collectively lost their goddamn minds. In under thirty years, we went from sending toy cars to Mars to magically disappearing and reappearing in every nook and cranny across the universe. We could colonize anywhere.

"If we can see it, we can reach it!" heralded recruitment videos populated by beautiful models who acted smart and awed with their black-rimmed glasses and stern gazes directed at distant worlds.

We'd stumbled into the Star Trek age before we even figured out how to make phasers.

And it all came down to the simple discovery of how easy it actually was to hack the Spacetime Continuum.

But more on that later. Let's get back to Flair, his office poster, his Armani suit, and his hardsale of seven years of isolation. Flair made the trip at forty-three years of age and, when he returned a multi-millionaire, he deemed it his life's mission to spread the good news to other candidates for the "adventure of a hundred lifetimes".

He talked in questions that didn't want answers. "Divorced, yeah? Your kids are both in college, yeah? You don't have any kind of real retirement, yeah? Tired of throwing away your time on these chicks that just wash up on your shore, just as hopeless as you, yeah? Take a look at that."

He jabbed his thumb toward a gold-framed wedding photo of him and a twenty-something brunette who was five inches taller than him. They both smiled big like they'd just pulled a fast one.

"Six years married to her. She was a stripper. You like strippers, yeah? Her name was Candy and that girl will do anything thing I ask to anyone I want. You like the sound of that, yeah? You go do this thing, you spend your seven years in space, you come back and you find a Candy, yeah? Hell, you got time tonight? Before we head out to the elevators, I'll take you out and show you how they treat men like us, the veterans. They know us, yeah? They know who we are the second we step back onto Earth. X-Verse only picks six escorts a year to take the Hotdog Machines across the universe, so when you come back, they know, mate. Every red hot piece of tail in town knows and they are gunning for you, yeah?"

I would be a multi-millionaire, I would miss my kids graduating college, maybe miss a marriage and the birth of a grandkid or two, but I'd be there for the rest. And I'd be rich. I'd give up my forties to have an easier fifties, sixties, seventies, and beyond. He didn't have to hardsell me on anything. I knew I would do it the second he announced himself on the phone two weeks ago. Men in my situation dreamed of this happening. The chance to do something significant, the chance to set myself up for life, and the chance of making my ex-wife boil in jealousy when she saw my own version of Candy clinging to my arm when I got back to Earth.

This was the California Gold Rush of my generation. Millions apply, some for permanent stays in space, but those like me get to come back. We just manage the resupply runs, short-timers compared to the scientists that go into the universe for a life sentence. I never really expected to get picked since no one is really sure what makes a man an ideal candidate for X-Verse aside from being 43 and single. I was beginning to suspect they looked for desperation, of which I had an ample supply.

"And I know you're gonna be perfect, mate. We don't mess with none of those young bucks, yeah? They got too much hormone, too much ego, not enough know how. No humility, yeah? But you, I know you, I know your type. You just get shit done. You're healthy, you work out, you eat right, you get shit done, yeah?"

For this he waited for an answer, and I gave him a sly smile and a shake of the head. It was a secret community. The middle-aged men who got shit done.

"My boy."

He pushed the contract toward me, motioned to a plastic hula dancer with a large silk flower sprouting from her head. I studied the hula dancer, then carefully pulled at the flower to reveal a pen lodged right down the center of her head. Once removed, the hula dancer began swaying her hips and singing.

Flair was pleased.

I signed away the better part of a decade to X-Verse and its mission to KOI-3284.01. My mission was to escort a new pod to replace an out-of-date model 1218 light years away. I will keep our species' most distant colony restocked and thriving.

"So, training?" I asked, perhaps too late. "How long will that last?"

"On the job training, my boy. You're shooting up tonight!"

Flair roared a rocket sound as his hand launched off his desk.

"So, we are or are not going to a strip club?"

1.2

A Community Pod resupply mission always takes seven years. Whether it is a trip to Jupiter or Betelgeuse, it is always seven years.

Flair attempted to explain the nuances of quantum physics and interstellar travel as he drove me in his fire-engine-red Maserati to the X-Verse corporate office in the Great Salt Plains in northern Oklahoma. I asked him if the salt would be a problem for his car and he shrugged.

"I'll buy a new one, yeah?"

The trick with space travel, Flair said, is scale. On our scale, reality is inflexible. An orange is an orange, a tree is a tree, if you went to sleep as a white man, you will wake up as a white man. But if you go small enough, reality is a mess. It's all in the chaos of the subatomic realm where anything is possible at any moment.

Or something, I don't know. Flair was drunk and getting drunker as he took pulls off a ruby-studded flask which was the even more ridiculous than his name.

"When you get itty bitty, matter can pop into life and pop out of life. All things are possible, my friend. An orange can be an apple, a tree could be a banjo, you can wake up a big-tittied black woman. Itty bitty, if there are no other outside factors, it's all chaos. But those itty bitty things are part of a bigger pattern and that pattern keeps the impossible from happening. But our scientists know how to use itty bitty tweezers to tweak itty bitty things to make oranges turn into apples and trees into banjos. Yeah?"

"No," I answered.

"Don't you worry too much about it. These scientists are just telling trillions and trillions of little atoms that make up your Hotdog Machine that they are no longer in one place and they are now in a place over a thousand light years away. They tell the little guys, the little guys believe them and they tell the universe and the universe believes the little guys."

Flair snapped his fingers.

"And there you are, my friend. Across the universe, like the Beatles song. Yeah?"

I knew something of the science from the casual reading I'd done during those first few years of X-Verse. Flair was right that, on the itty-bitty, reality is chaos, but the bigger reality get's, the more it stabilizes. The trick is to destabilize reality bit-by-bit, starting very small, then rebuilding it the way you want. You are hacking reality, telling the universe that something that was one way is now another way.

By hacking physics on the subatomic level, X-Verse is essentially taking the ship off the physical plane like they are God in a roomful of toys, and replacing it wherever they want it to be in the universe. The trip is instantaneous and near perfect. "Near" perfect. On one trip, only a quarter of the pod arrived and the entire crew was lost, some into the vacuum of space, and some in the process of tricking Timespace.

But that was one mission among dozens of others executed without a single hair out of place. Not bad odds, but did explain why finding worthy and willing candidates wasn't always easy.

When the program first began, the trips only took a couple of months as X-Verse moved supplies and crew onto the pods, then jumped from their Earth orbit. Each pod could house 160 people for over eight years without resupply thanks to a clever use of greenhouses and water capturing from alien planets, comets, asteroids, whatever. That eight years gave the crew plenty of time to investigate Earth-like planets and determine if a colony could be formed. If not, they snap their fingers and they are back to Earth.

After the lose of three-quarters of a Pod to the mystery of quantum hacking, the public grew nervous about the implications of X-Verse. In response, the company offered to extend their launching area out deeper into space. So, the trip is all about crawling far enough away from Earth that, if anything goes wrong, it'll just claim the lives of whoever is on board without dragging the Earth into the chaos.

There are greater implications to this like black holes and tears in the fabric of the Space/Time Continuum, but my understanding is mostly based on the Back to the Future trilogy, so I decided to just go with the flow and trust the scientists.

The elevator cables appeared over the Salt Plains as Flair talked about his partial ownership share of a semi-pro soccer team. I gazed up at the tall metal ropes, subtle waves rolling up the lines straight up into the sky like other-worldly dancers swaying with the wind.

The cables were one of the first wonders of X-Verse. There were eighteen elevators in the Salt Plains, constantly running up into space and back down to Earth, taking load after load after load. The Earth's spin kept the cables somewhat taught, another example of science fiction/fantasy turned reality by someone dumb enough to try and lucky enough to succeed. The elevators appeared small on the cables, but were actually the size of three train cars and could carry 15 ton loads. They blasted off the pad, then pushed up into space by an energy beam. It allowed X-Verse to build the Pods in space piecemeal, saving trillions in the process.

"Why so soon?" I asked. I signed the papers without questioning the immediacy of my placement. The wait list for Pod escorts was almost as long as the elevator cables, so I never actually thought I would make it in. I'd signed up on their website a couple years ago while drunk and mourning my latest heartbreak. I forgot all about my X-Verse application until Flair called me.

"Personnel issues. We needed someone, you fit the bill. You getting cold feet?"

"No, just curious."

"That's not why we hired you, to be curious, yeah?"

It was a bit of a threat, so I swallowed the rest of my questions and watched a elevator zip into the sky. I would be on one by the end of the day.

"And there's no chance my kids can come up to see me before I take off?"

I thought of my boys, the pictures hanging above the computer in my home office. They were just kids then, elementary school, their faces shifting, year-to-year, from toddler glee to middle school awkward cool. The terrible haircuts, the birthdays at arcades, the ridiculous kindergarten graduations with mini-caps and gowns.

They are in college. They don't need me. They don't need me.

"No chance, mate. Might as well get used to being alone at some point, yeah?"

"Way ahead of you."

1.3

Flair let me touch the elevator cable while we waited. It was cold, rigid, billions of nanotubes spun together in a tangle as wide as an oak tree trunk, but thin so it was more like an unwound ream of really thick duct tape. Above, the 23,000 foot cable plunged into the sea of clouds bursting with the warm splashes of color cast from the lush Oklahoma sunset. Somewhere beyond that was the docking station and the Community Pod. And far beyond that was the counterweight. And far, far beyond that was the infinite that would swallow me for seven years, then spit me back out as a rich man.

I'd been assigned a wardrobe of X-Verse-branded cotton t-shirts and sweatpants in various colors ranging from faded red to sky blue. I was not allowed to bring along my own clothes, my phone, or any other artifacts. My collection of photos, music, video games, and other entertainment were being loaded onto my personal hard drive on the ship, so the only physical thing I would bring was myself.

"When I was a kid, astronauts took years to train," I said, still gazing up along the length of the elevator cable. "I'm heading up there and still have no idea what I'm supposed to be doing."

"You aren't an astronaut, my friend," Flair said. "You are an escort. You aren't up there to measure things, to explain things, to figure things out. You are up there to be up there, to turn a ratchet when a nut get's loose or jam bubblegum into cracks in the hull. Your main job is not to go crazy, to do your time, and come home a rich bastard, yeah?"

"And if something goes really wrong?"

"You'll have all the help you need," Flair replied.

I turned and studied Flair. "But you said I'm going to be all alone up there."

"You are and you aren't."

The cable tremored and we both looked back at it.

"She's coming," Flair said. "Maybe another hour and you'll be lifting off. Let's get back inside."

***

The video monitor flashed pictures of both my boys. My oldest was flexing his bird-thin muscles while balancing on the shoulders of a statue. It was a football icon from his school who neither of us recognized. The other boy was biting into a gold medal he won during a chess tournament. The phone line rung in short blasts as it requested my boys pick up for a video conference. Neither did, which didn't surprise me. Just another nagging call from dad. They'd call me back when they were bored.

They had no idea what was happening. I didn't tell either of them about X-Verse in fear of jinxing my chances.

Now I was going to shoot up into space without being able to say "goodbye".

"Record Message?" flashed in big red letters.

"Yes."

A wavy line emerged to indicate my own vocal volume. I watched it weave to reflect the subtle white noise.

"Hey boys, it's your dad. I'm—"

I leaned back against the desk chair. X-Verse had installed me in a nameless, bland office tucked near the back of the launch station while they prepped the elevator. They gave me fifteen minutes for my call.

"Restart message."

The screen flashed, the once erratic line reborn as a gentle wave.

"I'm going to space to get rich boys! I'll be gone for seven years and it kills me that I won't be able to see you before I leave, but it was a last minute thing. I've been thinking of everything I needed to tell you or remind you of before I take off, but then I remembered that you are both far more responsible and capable than I ever was. You don't need me nearly as much as I need you.

"I'm gonna be gone for seven years. Seven years of not seeing you is the hardest thing I will ever do in my life and I cannot tell you how much it hurts right now, before I've even launched into space. But I will be back, and I will be rich and I will pay off your loans, buy your houses, meet your wives, maybe meet some grandkids. I am doing this for us.

"You will be able to send me messages and please, please, please do. I can't make it through this without your support. I need to know how you are doing. I need to know that you are okay. I know you will be because you are both smart and strong and clever and destined for great things. Just, keep me abreast.

"Don't worry about the house. X-Verse is packing everything up for me and will keep the place safe and sound. Maybe you can move in during the summers? I don't know. I'm sure something can be worked out. I quit my job, X-Verse is taking care of the bank accounts and my bills and all that. You don't have to do anything."

I didn't want to cry, but I was. They were slow tears, heavy and bull-headed.

"I'm gonna miss you both so bad. I hope you forgive me

for going. I'll make it up to you. I will. I promise. I'm going to make you proud, so you do the same for me, okay?

"End Message."

I sunk back into the chair and let the tears come fast and fierce. I don't cry often, I hate the way it feels, I hate the way it looks, I hate the way it sounds. But this one was okay, nobody could see and it needed to happen if I was going to survive.

***

I moved to the platform to get a better look at the elevator car. It was a cross between a flying saucer and a partially deflated volleyball. Futuristic, but not the glimmering and exciting future we all hoped for, but the disappointing and utilitarian future we all deserved.

But still, I was going to space, which lifted my spirits. I'd never have to go back to an office, I'd never have to mop another floor that I didn't own, I'd never have to date a woman I didn't want or couldn't afford. Everything was changing at the moment I stepped inside. A trillion dollar company chose me. They were trusting me with the most advanced technology ever created.

My sons would be proud of me as soon as they found out. They would brag to their friends, they would await my return, they would praise my name. My ex-wife's husband would feel like a piece of shit and my ex-wife would regret that she wasn't the one on my arm when I'm greeted home with acclaim, fortune, and so many strippers.

No. I won't do strippers. I'm better than that. Maybe some swimsuit models.

Flair waved me over to the edge of the platform where

he leaned against the railing. He pointed out toward the last gasp of the sunset.

"Enjoy it, yeah?"

We both folded our arms over the edge of the railing and gazed across the salt plains toward the blood red sliver of the sun about to drown in the horizon. The yellow and purple rays shot out like a child's last burst of happy energy before submitting to bedtime.

"This job is easy," Flair said. "The distance is hard. Just do what you're told. These people know their stuff, yeah? They've sent better people up there, they've sent worse people up there, all but one group made out okay. You are changing your entire family line, yeah? A thousand years from now, your name will pop out of the family tree like a Christmas light, but that bitch of an ex-wife won't even glimmer."

I smiled at that, but felt bad. She was still the mother of my boys. I wanted to be mad at Flair, I wanted to argue, but it felt good. It felt like I was winning. Every divorce was a competition. Who remarries better, who retires better, who is the favorite parent, who owns the favorite home. She was winning. For the last eight years, she was winning. But not now. Not once this elevator shoots up into the air. Flair understood me. I didn't like him, but I liked to be understood.

"She's a good woman," I finally said. "My ex-wife. We got divorced for a reason, but she is a good woman. Always was. She just went her way and I went mine."

Flair nodded, but didn't buy it. That made me feel good too because he didn't understand all of me. Flair wasn't the kind of person I wanted to completely understand me because that would make me like him. I'd be better when I got back. I wouldn't marry a stripper, I wouldn't waste my money on cars or suits. I'd be admirable. I'd be an art patron, I'd volunteer at schools, I'd be a community leader. I'd be the man I was always supposed to be.

"So, are you going or not?" a belabored worker called from the elevator.

Flair stood away from the railing and held out his hand. I shook it, held the grip tight while we smiled like brothers. Middle-aged men who got shit done.

I turned from him, nodded at the workers, stepped into the elevator and sat in a black recliner bolted to the floor. The captain's chair for my first leg of my life-defining journey.

The door slid closed, clamped shut. The rockets fired before I was ready. I shot into heaven.

1.4

Rocket propulsion, nausea, and fourteen hours of alone time followed.

An hour into the trip, a recorded video message popped up in mid-air, a couple feet above my eyes. There was no screen, just a projected image. A beautiful, caramel-skinned woman with a charming smile announced herself as "Esperanza Baker, the chief communications officer of the Bold Stride Community Pod."

"I am going to be introducing you to the exciting world of quantum re-writing and the Chaos Machine. You will not see me for another three years as I am in a Community Pod in a controlled orbit around KOI-3284.01. We call it 'Koi' for short, like the fish. Our staff will be assisting you in your functions as an escort for the next seven years. Once on your Community Pod, we will be linked to you via the Chaos Machine, so there will be no delay in our transmissions. As far as the universe knows, our signal might as well be transmitting from ten feet away. It is all very confusing, but we will try to make some sense of it over the next three years. I know it is a difficult concept to digest, but what drew X-Verse to you is your reputation for taking life at face value. Accepting the improbable is necessary for interstellar travel."

"And love," I responded, then wished someone was around to appreciate my cleverness.

Esperanza continued.

"There are a few daily functions you will need to perform, but mostly you will be on call in case there is an emergency that needs physical hands to fix. Perhaps the occasional hull puncture, a server reboot, all very straight-forward.

The Community Pods were designed to be simple and easy to repair. As long as the Chaos Machine is functioning, then we can walk you through just about anything.

"If the Chaos Machine goes down and can't be restarted, the Community Pod turns around automatically and heads home. And, just to get this out of the way early, do not even attempt to sabotage the Chaos Machine. We will know and you will not be paid for your time. X-Verse will sue you for any damage done. I know this was in your contract, but it bears repeating. Three years is a long transit time, so the thought will occur to you at some point. Just know that sabotaging the Chaos Machine will ruin your life. We will recover the damages from you and your descendants. But what is even more important, if you abandon your mission, I will die along with 159 other crew members. You are here now because an escort failed us. You have a little over three years to reach us before our greenhouses fail and our food supplies are exhausted. You are our only chance. There is no coming home for us, Will. We can't abandon our post and meet you halfway. We will stay at Koi no matter what. But it will all be okay because you will save us. You will be our hero. You will be my hero."

Her beautiful face faded into the X-Verse logo. I had the option of replaying the message. I did, three times, taking in the deep dimples in her cheeks, the bright, intelligent tone of her voice, the hazel eyes that dazzled like gemstones. She was directly within my strike zone. Ageless, eccentric, perhaps a tad unstable, but clever. Probably just as well that I would only have a few months with her cause I knew I'd just fuck it all up if I tried to date her.

I also knew myself well enough to know that I was going to still going to try. I liked the way "my hero" slipped through those beautiful lips.

I finally let the video projection fade away and settled back into my captain's chair. The elevator climbed at a staggered pace, something to do with friction and vibrations. The nanofibers in the cable were strong, but not impervious. The car responded to the cable like a lover, moving slowly when the cable needed to be caressed, racing when the cable grew stable and bored.

Seven years without sex. I spent an unhealthy amount of time guessing at what such a long dry spell would do to my physiology.

1.5

The Hotdog Machine glimmered in the sunlight, like a gilded cigar holder. Our link to the universe. Our hope for salvation because somewhere out there were the answers to global warming, to fuel shortages, to overpopulation, to our once-stalled destiny as God's greatest explorers.

So much hope for such a modest-looking thing. When we found other intelligent life, other interstellar travelers, would they mock our Community Pods? Were we riding the short buses? Or would they admire our ingenuity and humility, making so much out of so little? We didn't need to dress up our future, to primp and to pose. We were mutts who've slipped the collars of our home world, bounding out into open space with stupid enthusiasm and slobbery grins.

I couldn't be more proud to be a human.

PART 2

I woke to a fine orange mist spraying through my private chamber. The artificial sun was rising from the horizon in my room. It was an elaborate and gentle alarm clock sending rays across my bare, white walls. I heard a plastic squeak/groan, so glanced over at my white side table to see an orange on a cafeteria tray next to a bowl of oatmeal.

The orange was misshapen, slowly constricting as if being squeezed by invisible hands.

"Gossomer," I called into the empty room, my voice warped by a yawn sneaking out. "Gossmer!"

A projection glimmered and gathered into the shape of a red, furry beast with big, hopeful eyes, no discernible mouth, and cartoonish paws and feet. I motioned to my tray and his blue eyes followed, then widened as it saw the orange being squashed almost flat. The bowl holding the oatmeal cracked under the invisible strain.

A localized gravity malfunction.

Gossomer clapped its paws. I held onto my bunk as the artificial gravity shut off. The orange bounced off the tray as it popped back into its natural shape. I tracked it across the bedroom as I felt my back lift off the bunk. The oatmeal was floating up like a geyser. The mess was going to be horrible.

Such was life with quantum hacking. It was the science of making order out of chaos. It mostly worked great, but sometimes the chaos snuck through. Usually about once a day. At times, I yearned to just finish the trip without gravity, but Gossomer assured me that my body wouldn't hold up for the three years it took to reach the jump point.

So, how to explain artificial gravity? If you think instantaneous, cross-universe travel is confusing, hold onto your hats cause this is about to get stupid. Artificial gravity is another magical breakthrough thanks to the Chaos Machine. Early designs by other space agencies for artificial gravity involved massive wagon wheels and batons, all spinning through space to use centrifugal force to make up for the absence of a massive rock that we'd naturally stick to. Turns out that you don't really need all that nonsense. All you need is the will to control all the billions and billions of gravitons constantly flowing all around us. And the Chaos Machine has one heck of a will.

Esperanza did her best to break it down for me and then the Chief Science Officer, Dr. Hagin, gave it a stab. Here is the best metaphor I'd come up with to get my head around artificial gravity:

Think of gravitons as a massive flock of birds. Once spooked, those birds fly off in their own crazy ways, then resettle somewhere else, all finding their own usual places within the flock. We can disrupt the flock momentarily, but eventually it will always settle back to where it is supposed to be, kinda evening out like water.

Something as big as a planet will cause the flock to concentrate in that one area, increasing gravity.

But we don't have a planet, so X-Verse needed a new way. They discovered that just getting the birds flying could have the same desired effect. Spook the flock, over and over and over again, get them flying in crazy patterns, scattering for safety or to find better, safer patches of land. Then, lasso each one of those birds and make them all flap out in the same directions, Viola! I stick the ground.

The Chaos Machine uses these tiny Big Bangs to create and disrupt gravitons, forcing them to unsettle, then lassoing them all, pulling them into a formation to concentrate all their energy on creating an artificial gravity within the ship. The Chaos Machine continually goes through this process, millions of mini-Booms in a minute to make sure that the attraction between my feet and the ship's hull remains steady, engaged.

Gossamar watched the geyser of oatmeal and ricocheting orange, then looked to me, apology rich in his big, sad eyes. He clapped his furry hands again. Gravity eased back on, its strength gaining, easing me back down to the bunk. The orange's flight slowed, bowed, arched down to the ground. The oatmeal spilled out across my side table.

Gossomer rose its furry arms in panic, its eyes alarmed, then pressed its paws to the side of its head.

"It's okay, I got it," I reassured Gossomer.

Gossomer straightened formally, like a concierge. A word bubble rose above its head reading "Would you like me to prepare another breakfast?"

"I'll be fine, but thank you."

I waved him away and he disappeared. Gossomer once had a speech function, but it annoyed me. The voice was elegant and a tad uppity, like the HAL 9000. I told Gossomer I would only respond to him if he spoke in the form of speech bubbles à la comic books. He obliged and now we get along famously. Sixty percent of my job satisfaction was derived from frustrating that poor, little fellow.

I looked over the cooling oatmeal splattered across my room. It would have to wait. I needed to check the Chaos Machine. Protocol dictated that I examine the Chaos Machine for anything out of the ordinary following every reset. I pulled on my sweatpants, t-shirt, and slippers, then left my private chambers.

I slept, ate, and lived most of my life in Tube 5, but the

Chaos Machine was located in Tube 3, the center of the Community Pod. I only had full access to tubes 4 and 5. Tube 4 contained the showers, workout rooms, various work labs, and supplies. Tube 5 contained private chambers, all unoccupied aside from mine. Tube 3 housed the mess hall and the greenhouses. I had access to only one greenhouse which had become my own private Eden. Everything past the Chaos Machine was off limits. Gossomer told me that X-Verse wanted to keep the rest of the Community Pod sealed off and in perfect, uncontaminated condition so, no matter how disgusting I might be, at least half of the ship was immediately livable once I arrived at Koi. Maybe there were mutant humans enhanced for deep space explorations, or nuclear warheads for a battle with the planet's inhabitants resisting our colonization. Who knows? Who cares?

I tried sneaking over to Tube 2 once, not out of curiosity, but just to see what would happen. Gossomer appeared in front of the hatch with seriously frowny eyeballs and a lot of exclamation points.

As I exited my private chambers for my morning stroll to the Chaos Machine, I saw a pleasant warm mauve splashed across the walls.

"Gossomer!" I called.

He appeared, eyebrows arched in eager expectation, clapping his paws.

"Turn it back," I said.

His eyebrows fell, disappointed. A word bubble read: "Studies show that warm colors increase overall mental well-being while in deep space transit."

"I don't care, turn it back."

Gossomer hesitated. He bowed his head, then clapped,

this time like a defeated genie. The tubes flashed to the original uniform, institutional white. We went through this every morning, him trying a different color, me ordering him to move it back to white. Of course, white was hideous, but I also didn't like Gossomer forcing things on me. And I liked to annoy him. I no longer had a wife, children, or dogs to harass, so Gossomer had to absorb all of my puckishness. I'd give in one day, but only at that moment that I'd frustrated him to the point that I feared him opening up an airlock.

The tubes were long, about two hundred yards each, so winding through the Hotdog Machine took time. In the initial weeks of my trip, I'd sprint at top speed to the Chaos Machine, fearing the worst. Most anomalies were just gravity disruptions, but there were the more elaborate hiccups in quantum hacking.

The most terrifying anomalies so far:

1. A severed animal arm with talons, still twitching, confused as to where its owner went. I bagged that one up and stored it in the deep freeze so the scientists could examine it later.

2. Shimmering bubbles floating in the mess hall, about the size of softballs. I searched for a malfunctioning dishwasher for about ten minutes until one of the bubbles clunked me in the head. It was as hard as glass.

3. A disembodied singing female voice. She sounded so sad, wherever she was. I thought it was from the sound system, but realized it was real, breathy, not condensed and digital. I was deeply unnerved until Gossomer assured me it was a glitch. He reset the Chaos Machine and, sure enough, the voice was gone. My ghost vanquished, the closest thing I'd had to personal contact since I left Earth.

The anomalies became something like routine and the days that the Chaos Machine didn't glitch out worried me more, like a roomful of children that suddenly got too quiet.

I took my time that day, grinning happily to Gossomer as he led me onward, goading me with wild arm waves to move faster.

The smattering of science labs and office cubicles with low walls lining Tube 4 had long gaping windows so administrators could glare in to make sure the pions were hard at work. They lit up every day, even though they would remain unused for another three years.

Gossomer was at the end of the hall, arms folded, tapping his toes, glaring at me. I stopped, folded my arms and tapped my toes, glaring at him. He watched me confused, realized I was mocking him, then waved his arms, motioning me on.

Tube 3 contained the only colors in the Community Pod, with the lush greenhouses bursting with all manner of life. Flowers, fruits, vegetables, all set up in high density gardens, all carefully picked for nutrition and/or crew members' mental well-being. Misters hissed on from time to time. I was to only enter my own greenhouse twice a day so as not to let the vapor escape. Water was precious and wasn't as efficiently captured out of the air in the rest of the tubes as it was in the greenhouses. The rest of the greenhouses were maintained by little robots that looked and moved like industrious spider monkeys, their fur replaced with white and black plastic. Their eyes were big, like Gossomer's, but with glassy lenses that examined everything, including the dark depths of my soul.

Gossomer wouldn't let me have one as a pet.

Beyond the greenhouses was the Chaos Machine and

the end of my territory. Gossomer waited by the door, arms folded again. A thought bubble above his head only read "........."

I mimicked a kiss to his cheek, which he bitterly accepted.

Inside, the room was dark save the glowing Chaos Machine. I was technically in charge of the seven-foot-tall, shimmering hope for all of mankind with its thousands of tiny little big bangs bursting in every color of the universe, spewing out little galaxies and stars that soon collapsed back into tiny black holes only to burst out again.

It was like a fireworks display and/or a trippy screen-saver trapped inside the glass tube. And this impossible thing was my responsibility. I had a checklist. I was given a thorough explanation of maintenance by a brittle old man named Dr. Hagin. He diligently went over every little aspect of the Chaos Machine and all the little things that could be performed should a major issue arise. In truth, I had no idea what I was looking for whenever I went over the checklist since Dr. Hagin, despite his thoroughness on the machine's uses and innards, was not clear when it came time to explaining what normal/abnormal looked like. I suspected he didn't know himself.

The room containing the Chaos Machine was small, barely bigger than a walk-in closet. It was the only dark room in the Community Pod, only illuminated by a small reading light trained over a big, red reset button and the bursts of light glowing out from the Chaos Machine. So far, I'd had no need for the reset button since Gossomer could always reset it for me. But if he failed, then I had to hustle my butt across the Pod and slap that button like I was trying to stop the countdown for armageddon.

Cause, for me, a malfunctioning Chaos Machine was armageddon.

Inside that incomprehensible wonder of quantum hacking were trillions of micro Big Bangs happening over and over and over and over again, allowing the Chaos Machine to mold reality. It was mesmerizing and indecipherable, like magic. True magic.

I unhooked a small digital pad next to the machine and the checklist appeared. I hit "Yes" on all the buttons without considering what question I was answering. As long as gravity worked and the lights were on, I figured we were all good.

"How is everything?" a voice emerged, like a playful whisper in my ear.

"Fine as cherry wine, darling," I replied, imagining Esperanza's hazel eyes, a slight arch in her right eyebrow, her lips almost smiling, almost flirting.

"Another malfunction?" she asked.

"Of course, cost me my breakfast."

"Poor Will."

I replaced the digital pad, kissed my fingers and pressed the kiss on the glass of the Chaos Machine. Little sparks of light sped to the glass. Chaos kissing me back.

"Yes, poor me."

"Don't worry," Esperanza said. "She is just stretching her legs, give her time to settle in. It will get better. Wanna watch a movie tonight?"

Her question annoyed me. I knew I had to say "yes", condemning me to two hours making snide comments about whatever stupid movie she chose. I'd force giggles and mild flirtations, but we would know that the night was as flavorless and meaningless as unbuttered popcorn. Long distance relationships were just not my thing. The newness was long gone and all I was left with was a sense of obligation. I couldn't keep it up for another three years.

I knew I would eventually push her away and choose to just be alone. But then that would get old and I would try to get her back. Repeat that again and again over the course of three to seven years.

Plus, deep in my skull was the fear that she was just flirting with me to keep me engaged with the mission, to give me a reason to carry on. If I abandoned the mission, she would die. I would never do that, of course, but she didn't know that. She just knew me as another over-the-hill guy taking one last grasp at relevance.

"Sure," I answered, finally.

2.2

Gossomer's squat, thick-shouldered frame was not well-suited to jumping jacks, which absolutely delighted me. Every fifteenth set, he would bend over, pant, wipe sweat from his brow, then unleash a thought cloud containing censored cuss words such as "@%&" and "#$#k you, Will!"

I insisted on that too. Both the cuss words and that they are censored.

From thin air came Esperanza's whispering purr of "Hey handsome."

"Hey tootsie pop." I was immediately aware that I may have inadvertently said something racist. She giggled, so I assumed I was in the clear.

I knew why she was calling me. When I was in a particularly obstinate mood, Gossomer would notify Esperanza who would then intervene and talk me into doing whatever I was supposed to be doing. In this case, go workout. I wasn't opposed to physical exertion. I liked jogging. I liked having a toned body and looking palatable naked, but isolation sapped my motivation and all I wanted to do anymore was torture poor Gossomer.

I told him if he did a thousand jumping jacks, I would go run three miles. I planned on making him do another thousand pull ups before I would agree to weight training.

I explained to Gossomer that I was traumatized by finding a beating heart in Tube 2 that morning. Another glitch. It was only pumping air, like a gasping fish. It looked human, but my knowledge of the dimensions of the human heart was limited to my brother's insistence that it was the size of a closed fist. He also told me that if my hand was bigger than my face, I had cancer. Then he made me slap myself.

The sight of the beating heart did unnerve me, especially since the heart could have been plucked from a hapless stranger who was going about his day, maybe holding hands with his beloved while walking through a serene park on a perfect day. In his right hand was half of a loaf of bread, ready to be picked and thrown to the ducks. In his left hand, his darling, little woman with beaming smile, red lipstick a bit too intense for such a fair face, but he never minded.

He would take a few steps, baffled by the sudden panic of his body searching for the organ that was just there. He would try to carry on, not wanting to frighten her, not wanting to ruin such a perfect afternoon. Maybe she was pregnant, maybe they had kids.

He would fall over, death coming quick as his brain depleted the last of the oxygen. Lights out. Her scream never reached his ears.

Or maybe the heart came from an elk or from something from a different part of the universe or the Chaos Machine just spit it out from thin air. A random, miraculous, but meaningless conception.

The heart was gone now and I wasn't really too concerned about the anomalies implications. I picked at the thought, like the bread for the ducks, tossing it to my starved brain cells now months removed from human contact and fresh stimulation.

"So, whatcha doing?" Her voice was light, but I could tell she knew what was happening.

"You're a snitch," I called to Gossomer. He stopped doing jumping jacks and flipped me off, a blurry censor bar covering his hand. He was getting feisty.

"You need to stop torturing Gossomer or he is going to

snap and flush your ass out into space," Esperanza said.

"Challenge accepted."

I leaned up off my bunk and retrieved my socks and running shoes. Gossomer bent over, gasping for breath and tracking me with blood-shot eyes.

"I didn't say stop," I instructed as I pulled on the socks.

"I have a present for you," Esperanza said.

"Is it a human heart? I hope not 'cause someone already got me one."

"No, silly. It's even better."

There was a tapping at my door. I pulled on my running shoes, then crossed around Gossomer to tap the Open button.

Outside, a spider monkey robot held a metallic band with LED lights on the ends. It looked like a Caesar crown, but thinner. I took the band and waved the robot away, allowing the door to close behind me. Gossomer watched as he continued his jumping jacks.

"It's called a Halo," Esperanza said. "The lights go at your temple, the band fitting around the back of your head."

"I'm not really a hat guy."

"Stop being a dick, just put it on."

As I slipped it around my head, I felt a mild electrical current tickling my temples.

"Is this for migraines or something?" I asked.

Another tap at the door.

"Christ, do you want a tip or something?" I called.

Another tap.

With a sigh, I smacked the Open button.

Over a dozen humans were standing at my door.

I screamed. I tripped backwards into my room. The door slid shut just as the laughter erupted.

I pulled a pillow around and held it in front of my chest. What I hoped the pillow would accomplish, I cannot say.

The door opened again. I recognized Esperanza. She was shorter than I imagined, but there was no mistaking those hazel eyes and plump lips. That almost smile. Then Dr. Hagin, frail, thin, but with clever eyes shining like the only bright lights in a very dark world.

"What the hell?" I stammered.

"Welcome to Koi," Dr. Hagin announced. "Or at least welcome to our orbit above Koi."

"What the hell?"

"Sorry if we scared you," Dr. Hagin said, taking a step into my chambers. I held up the pillow as if it was a Spartan shield. "We don't often get to prank new people, so we appreciate this unique opportunity."

"What the hell?"

"We aren't real, Will," Esperanza said, smiling. She followed Dr. Weinke into the room. "We are just projections. It's the Halo, it allows you to see our Community Pod and we can see into yours. Since every Community Pod has the same design, this allows us to interact with crew from all across the universe as if we were all in one ship."

"You've been watching me?" I asked.

"Of course," Dr. Hagin said.

"The whole time?"

"Yes, Will." Dr. Hagin said. "We all think you are quite a wonderful dancer."

Two weeks ago I may have gotten a little stir crazy. There was toilet paper and interpretive dance involved.

The others chuckled behind Dr. Hagin.

"We'd hesitated giving you the Halo because we were having so much fun watching you be you," Esperanza said. "But we began to feel bad. Also, you should wear clothes more often."

That could be a reference to many things. So many things.

"What the hell?"

"Dr. Hagin, can you give us a second?" Esperanza kept her eyes on me, her almost smile infuriating me, but also about the most charming thing I'd ever seen. My body and mind were tugging in too many different directions.

"Of course," the old man said with a bow. He walked out the door and it slid shut.

Esperanza knelt down in front of me.

"I'm sorry, darling," she whispered. "I know it is a lot to take in, but I could tell you were struggling, so I thought this might help. Some escorts never get to know about the Halo because us pilgrims like our privacy and some of the other escorts are pretty damn creepy. But I like you and I didn't like watching you be so lonely."

I took her in, her smooth skin, the slight grit to the timbre of her voice, the way age left gentle lines around her smile like pretty little question marks.

"We use the Halos to talk to other Community Pods across the universe," she said. "It helps us not feel so alone. Also, there is this."

She reached her hand up to her temple, tapping against the LED lights. They went from blue to green. I felt the gentle buzz in my temples intensify. She leaned close to me. I noticed a static wave, like air, moving around me. I could smell shampoo, a touch of citrus and rose.

Then her lips pressed against my forehead. Electric, real. Almost real. Real enough. My body surged and glowed, catching my breath. Touch.

"What the hell?" I gasped, barely a whisper. I was aware at how much I was sweating. My nostrils flared, grasping for more of her scent.

Esperanza leaned away, tapped the Halo again, the light shifting back to blue. The buzz eased. She stood up and turned for the door. She looked back over her shoulder, her entire body in this beautiful, gentle twist.

"Ready to meet the others?"

I felt myself nod dumbly and push to my feet. My brain was cloudy. My palms clammy like a teenager's.

The door slid open and the crowd parted, allowing Esperanza to guide me out amid them. Faces. Faces. Faces. Mostly my age, some older, some men, some women. It was a lot to take in. Too much to take in. My eyes kept trailing back to Esperanza. Dr. Hagin's hand reached out for mine, his Halo glowing green. My nostrils caught a piney deodorant, something savory like licorice or long-faded pipe smoke. I reached for his hand, feeling the static and the impression of flesh. Not quite real, but my hand gripped his all the same.

I laughed like an astonished child. The others laughed. With me this time.

Names bounced against me as people were introduced. Lots of them had "doctor" affixed to the front. I absorbed nothing.

"And that is why I wanted to talk to you about the Chaos Machine," a voice was saying. I'd tuned in too late. She was in her mid-fifties. Pretty, thin, a gray streak among her black hair placed too precisely to be unintentional.

"Sorry, why?" I asked.

"The anomalies. There have been more than usual and we will need to figure out why," she said with a patient and practiced smile. "When you have time, of course."

I nodded.

I felt a hand on my shoulder and I turned to find Esperanza. My nose wrinkled, finding her scent again. I wanted to kiss her. She introduced another new face. I didn't catch the name, but something about decoration. I think there was another "Dr." involved in his name.

"You can't do these white walls anymore," he said.

"You sound like Gossomer," I replied, then looked for the little red guy. He waved with big, happy eyes.

"Aren't you supposed to be doing something?" I said.

A question mark appeared in a thought bubble. His shoulders stooped, then he resumed his jumping jacks.

I realized the doctor decorator was still talking.

"...long-term emotional stability. I'd suggest light blues, but we could stay with white if we put up some art and accent pieces. Anything to break up the monotony."

I was nodding my head, not really understanding what I was agreeing to. I just wanted this moment to end so I could lure Esperanza back into my room, alone, our Halos glowing green.

Noise rose over Doctor Decorator's voice. He grew silent, the crowd followed my gaze down the tube where rapid footsteps approached.

A woman emerged, slowing from her run. Her eyes locked onto mine. She was panting. Her eyes wide, stunned. She was beautiful. Thin, short, her light blonde hair hanging down in messy curls, face sculpted, perfect and charismatic.

A touch of tomboy to her stance. Maybe a dancer. Maybe a fighter. Probably both.

A young, handsome man broke from the crowd and jogged towards her. The woman didn't track him, instead keeping her eyes on me. When the man reached her, he started whispering. All eyes were on the woman aside from Esperanza's. She was busy watching me. I shot Esperanza a questioning shrug. She frowned, looked to the woman who was arguing with the man without looking at him. I guessed he was a boyfriend of some sort, trying to talk her down as she continued staring at me. I was tempted to wave, hoping to ease the tension.

The woman finally backed away, turned and stormed back into Tube 4.

"Is that another practical joke?" I asked.

Nervous chuckles emerged within the crowd.

"No, that was Kiersten," Dr. Hagin said. "She is the finest engineer I have ever worked with. Unfortunately, her mind is like a million bouncey balls dropped from a five-story building onto a highway during rush hour."

"Ah."

"You will stay away from Kiersten," Dr. Hagin said, firmly. "Trust me, Will. You don't want any part of her."

But I did. A million bouncy balls falling onto a highway during rush hour sounded like the most fantastic thing. I had to see what that meant. She was one of those girls you know the second you see her. Not everything of course, but you see that your future would bend toward her, no matter what anyone did about it. Her's was a gravity that couldn't be faked or fought. I would gladly fall into her even if it might destroy me. Especially if it might destroy me.

2.3

All that said, Esperanza looked fabulous on a treadmill. She had that perfect balance of curves and tone. Every step brought waves and shifts, tapping into the deepest of deep instinctual sparks deep in my core.

That mysterious girl still haunted me, but she'd become a distant shadow while I watched Esperanza's body perform.

The bargain with Esperanza was this: I get the Halo so as long as I start behaving like a professional interstellar transit escort. With the Halo comes community, something I was really suffering without.

We didn't discuss Kiersten, we didn't discuss Gossomer, or me dancing naked with rolls of toilet paper streaming out behind me. We just ran and enjoyed proximity, or at least artificial proximity.

The Halo was quite comfortable. Snug without being tight. It didn't jostle as I moved, but didn't squeeze my temples like an undersized ball cap. I kept wanting to reach from my treadmill to hers, just to touch her skin. My mind couldn't process what was happening and just wanted to feel, feel, feel, feel. She was an unfinished song looped in my mind, a touchstone that just needed to be worried enough that I finally could understand this new existence.

After the workout, I was halfway into the women's shower before I realized I had to start behaving like a civilized human being again. I turned around and made my way to the men's. I suddenly became very self-conscious, not wanting to remove the Halo on the chance that some pervert might be watching me while I couldn't watch him. I then wondered if Esperanza had ever watched me shower.

Or Kiersten.

It was all giving me a terrible headache so I hurried through my shower, scurried back to my chambers and turned out the lights. I thought about removing the Halo, but was terrified that someone would sneak in on me and glare down on my defenseless form with murder in their eyeballs.

Hours passed like this. Me hiding in my room, my headache pulsing like an angry vein, sounds of passing crew members. Then shuffling feet, uncertain feet. A tap on the door. I ignored it, not really certain why I was hiding anymore, but now embarrassed that I'd been hiding out so long. Shame and fear feeding off one another. I felt a hollowness in my stomach and guessed dinnertime had come and gone.

Gossomer emerged in my darkened room, sending off his red glow across the walls. A speech bubble announced "Esperanza is at your door. You should let her in."

"Is she mad?" I asked Gossomer.

"She is worried," his bubble read. Gossomer looked worried too, with crescents at the tops of his eyes and scrunched eyebrows.

"Tell her I am fine and that I just needed time to get my bearings."

"Tell her yourself," Gossomer said, his right eyebrow lifting in conspiracy.

I knew what that meant.

"Okay, let her in then make yourself scarce."

***

It was wonderful, by the way. Not perfect. There was no real weight to it, no real resistance. Flesh wasn't flesh, but it was close and satisfying in its own way. It sparkled, like tiny fireworks all over. Static stings from a wool sweater, just it stabbed in all the right places. It was also awkward for what it wasn't. She wasn't really there, after all, so allowances had to be made.

She slept next to me that night. I breathed her in, marveling at how wonderful women smell. So mystifying. So different. I wanted to wake her up, stir her up.

Yes, the weight on the bed wasn't right, she couldn't curl on top of me, couldn't cuddle, couldn't use me as a pillow, which made me a little lonely. Finally, I removed the Halo halfway through the night, feeling it to be more of a distraction that kept me from sleep, but then put it back on in fear that Esperanza would view removing the Halo as an abandonment.

I never really slept, but I still rose in the morning in my best mood in months.

We decided to stagger our trips to the mess hall.

"Everyone knows, of course, but still," she said, dressing while I studied her body, comparing it to all the other women I'd seen naked. It was a horrible habit, I admit, but also unavoidable. I assumed she did the same to me, which is why I leaned on one elbow in the bed, facing her to make my shoulders seem wider.

"We should do this again," she said, smiling back at me.

"Yes."

An awkward silence resumed. There was much to discuss. Was she doing this with other people on other Community Pods? Was I one of many or were we coupled for at least the next three years until I turned for home? What happened if we got tired of one another?

And who the hell was Kiersten?

Of course I couldn't ask her that, but the other questions would need to be addressed at some point.

The moment she left, I summoned Gossomer. He appeared, pleased with me. I imagined he wanted to gossip, ask me if I loved her sooooo much.

"Can you hide me from the other crew so they can't see or hear me?" I asked.

His speech bubble said "yes, but I can override it if I think you are in trouble."

Then his eyes narrowed as he tacked on: "Or getting into trouble."

I wanted to make him do push-ups, but resisted.

"Let's run silent, then," I said, wishing I could do a passable Sean Connery impression.

Gossomer clapped his hands. I took off my Halo and put it on the side table, hoping he wasn't lying to me. How horrible would that be? And none of those fuckers would say a damn thing.

"Can I look at their personnel files?" I asked, standing to get dressed.

The question surprised Gossomer and he studied me, maybe waiting for a punch line.

"Yes or no?"

"Yes," Gossomer said in his speech bubble while his eyebrows were sharp with skepticism.

"Check out Kiersten's," I said. "I don't know her last name, but she's blonde. And pretty. Super pretty."

"Will!" his speech bubble screamed.

"I didn't ask for you to moralize, just do what I say or I'm going to shave you and wear your fur as a beard."

His eyes narrowed. My eyes narrowed. It was a stand off.

His speech bubble emerged.

"Fine. How do you spell the name?"

"I have no idea. Just look through the 'K's. There can't be that many deviations. Show me pictures and I'll tell you when I see her."

Gossomer folded his arms and put his paw to his chin, thinking. He snapped his fingers, then pointed to the air next to him. A grid of profile pictures appeared. Seven women, none of them were the bouncy ball woman.

"That's all the 'K's?"

Gossomer nodded.

"Bring up the rest of the women."

The grid expanded to wrap across the walls. I turned, searched the faces, but didn't find her.

"Is it possible that they might not let me see her file?"

Gossomer nodded.

"Can you show it to me anyway."

Gossomer shook his head "No" with smiling eyebrows.

"You are not my friend anymore."

2.4

I tried the Halo in the morning. I really tried. The walls were now a light blue. "Stillwater" according to doctor decorator. I didn't argue, nor did I voice my apprehension of a series of flower paintings he had planned. I just thanked him and went to the mess hall. I'd decided to eat with crew members instead of having the spider monkey bring it to me like the weirdest, cutest little butler in the entire universe. They asked me about my boys. I recounted the messages they'd sent, reporting football scores, movie buzz, funny stories from the restaurant the oldest boy worked out. The youngest strongly implied that my plan to create a skate park inside my mansion was pure idiocy.

Whatever. He'd always been a stick in the mud.

My boys rarely told me about their grades or if they were dating anyone. They seemed okay with my decision to leave. Not happy. Not sad. Just okay. The crew members were genuinely pleased with this, which pleased me.

I then walked the halls, nodding at all the new faces, dropping into conversations with whoever was loitering outside of science labs, not making it too obvious I was always looking for Keirsten.

I then began to wonder if I would be able to spot anomalies as easily with all these projections around. Then wondered, not for the first time, what would happen if I just let an anomaly exist. I thought about finding the grey-streaked hair woman so I could ask her.

Then the panic hit. It was triggered by walking into a hall where a crowd congregated. All the voices, all the bodies making the tube feel small, packed. It felt like a runaway train, rumbling faster and faster.

I was sweating. The crowd turned toward me and I feared I had said something out loud.

I slipped off the Halo, the crowd evaporated, a severe headache suddenly rising to the surface. I retreated back to my chambers. I looked into my room, seeing the empty space, wondering if a ghost was filling that space. My breaths were coming fast.

"Gossomer!"

He appeared inside the room. I closed the door behind me.

"Am I alone?"

"Yes," his bubble announced as he looked around, confused.

"Like, really alone?"

"Yes…?"

I now hated the speech bubble.

I left the Halo on the side table, threw the blankets over my head and ordered Gossomer to mute the universe so I could hide inside my fortress of solitude. The ship that once felt so big now was infested with eyes, footfalls, and sounds. There were too many jokes that I was not included in, too many explanations that I wouldn't understand. Alienation.

Time passed. An embarrassing amount of time. I wanted to leave my bed, but was now afraid of how they would look at me if I threw my Halo back on. Or how they were looking at me without the Halo. They could have been in my room. The entire ship, packed in, staring down at me, taking bets on how long it would take before I either got up or wet the bed.

"Is anyone in here Gossomer?" I asked

I peeked above the covers at him, sitting on an invisible chair floating in the air. His head was craned backward, his arms limp at his side, his speech bubble reading "ZZZZZZZZZZ"

"Gossomer!"

Gossomer startled and leaned up quickly, his bloodshot eyes blinking the sleep out.

"Is there anyone in her right now?"

Gossomer speech bubble read "???"

He looked around the room, then shrugged.

"No, I mean, from the other ship. Like, their projection or whatever?"

Gossomer pointed to my side table.

"Esperanza?" I looked to the empty space where I guessed she was sitting.

Gossomer nodded.

"Okay. Unmute."

"Baby, how are you?" her voice emerged.

"A little freaked out." The sheets were still up to my nose. "But I will be okay. It's a bit of a transition, you know?"

"I can imagine. You take your time. If there is anything I can do."

Her voice carried an implied invitation. I looked to the Halo, considered.

"You kinda feel like a babysitter to me," I said.

"Wow. You've had some fucked up babysitter experiences."

"No, I mean, not like that. Not the sex part, but—are you here because you want to be or because you are my minder?"

She didn't answer immediately. I wanted to pull the sheets back over my head. I knew the question was a mistake.

"Are you implying that I am a whore?"

It was a smack to the face, the way she asked it. I hurt her, she hurt me back. I hated relationships for moments like these. There was no backtracking. That statement would hang between us forever.

"No," I said, knowing that it was too late. "I am just overwhelmed. I'm not sure what is going on in my head, but I guess I feel a little violated and humiliated and claustrophobic. I thought the ship was empty."

"It is, but we have to keep an eye on you, Will. I shouldn't have given you the Halo but, I don't know. I like you and I wanted you to feel less alone. And I wanted to be closer to you. I didn't do it because anyone was pushing me into bed with you. I think you are handsome and funny and kind."

"We will only have six months together," I said. The sheets came down. I wanted to see her face, so I grabbed the Halo. The buzz tickled my temples, her image appeared, sitting just a few feet from me. I felt her presence, the way she filled the room in her ship on the other side of the universe.

And those eyes that I couldn't quite meet.

"From the time I finally arrive and we actually meet," I continued. "We will have six months, then I will never see you again. We will go from Halos to Real back to Halos and then to Nothing. It will be a series of breakups."

"It's not easy," she said, her beautiful eyes sad trying to find mine, but not able to hold on and drifting back to her hands. "These arrangements are hard, but it is all we have. I can't afford to have real sex and risk getting pregnant or, just as bad, developing a toxic relationship with someone

I will share a ship with for the rest of my life. So, this is it for me. We actually have a dating community where you can meet people from other ships, just so there is always someone new. Always more fish in the ether. Fake sex is still better than no sex. Touch is touch."

"Not really," I said.

"No, not really. I'm sorry, Will. I should have left you alone. I should have kept it professional. I was trying to help and, well, I was curious."

I sat up in bed. I felt better, which was horrible because I could see Esperanza was struggling, but that was one less complication for me to deal with. I liked her, I really, really did, but there was no future. With everything else I needed to digest and process, I had felt buried. With her sorted, I felt better about reentering society.

"Thank you for being patient with me," I finally said. I considered kissing her on the cheek or something sweet like that, but decided against it. The moment was heavy for her and I didn't know how she would react.

Esperanza nodded, stood, and turned for the door. It hissed open and I saw a painting of a tall, bursting sunflower on the opposite wall. It leaned forward like it was trying to reach across the hall to gaze inside my bedroom.

"If you feel up to it," Esperanza began. "Dr. Aker needs to discuss the Chaos Machine."

"Who is that? Did I meet her yesterday?"

"She is the one with the black hair and gray streak."

"Ah. Okay. Tell her I am on my way."

I stood, grabbed my clothes, but paused.

"Does everyone think I am a nutcase? Are they going to be staring at me?"

Esperanza chuckled and turned to me.

"Honey, after everything we've seen you do over the last three months, hiding in bed is nothing."

***

I found a herd of vibrating jelly beans. They were migrating across Tube 4 on the way to the Tube 3, skittering across the floor rather than rolling. Some miracle of the Chaos Machine making this form of locomotion more efficient than the age old wheel-based technology.

I suspected they were after the plants in the greenhouses, the poor hungry things.

I was tempted to touch one of the black jelly beans, just to see if it was indeed a real jelly bean. Everyone else hates black jelly beans, but I've always had a soft spot for them. I identified with the outcast jelly bean. So intense, so bracing. You earned the rest of the bag of jelly beans by eating the black jelly beans, a rite of passage, an acquired taste. I once dated a girl that often hung out in my room, naked, curled against me, eating jelly beans, and bitching about the world. She made me eat her black jelly beans, which I did eagerly, my way to consume her love. She was my own black jelly bean.

I stepped over the herd, deciding to let the jelly beans exist for a few more minutes as I sought out Dr. Aker, the woman with the bold gray stripe in her hair and the sharp face that held onto a beauty that was beyond the erosion of time. She'd make a great politician's wife. Instead she chose space. An eternity of isolation. Maybe she was escaping an abusive lover or a harsh mother figure. I assumed all explorers were running from something, seeking out new lands so they can escape the old.

Dr. Aker talked a lot, meeting me with a stern and urgent wall of information regarding the poorly performing Chaos Machine. Her words swept by too fast to follow. She rarely even stopped to breathe, like she'd developed some process of constantly taking in air from her nose while emitting nonsensical technical jargon from her mouth. I wanted to record her and play theses three minute long sentences back to her so she could get an idea of how damn ridiculous she was.

I then began to suspect she grew up in a domineering, male-dominated family and her only defense was a relentless storm of sound, wearing down the bigger, stronger brothers through ceaseless nags. I pictured her as jabbering crow on the back of a weary mule, driving it forward through caws, squawks, and beak jabs. This made me smile.

Then I was aware that several moments of silence had passed. She was looking at me while holding a stethoscope to the Chaos Machine as if she was listening to its heartbeat. Little sparkling stars danced around where the bell of the stethoscope was placed against the glass. I waited, but then she raised her eyebrows at me. She must have asked a question.

"I'm gonna be honest," I said. "I don't know anything about whatever it is that is happening right now. I do know that I just walked past a herd of living jelly beans and that is probably not supposed to be a thing. Don't bother explaining to me what is wrong. Just tell me what you need from me."

She lowered the stethoscope, took the ends out of her ears and let it hang from her neck. I spent time thinking about how a stethoscope was helpful when she was really just listening to their Chaos Machine on their ship light years away instead of mine. I considered asking, but couldn't stand to listen to her tsunami of explanation.

Dr. Aker was still silent. I'd frustrated her to the point that she was simply looking at me like I was a puppy that couldn't grasp the concept of shitting outside the house.

"I'm not a scientist." I felt even more dumb having to explain that.

"But you can listen to what I am telling you?"

I thought about answering "no." Instead I just nodded my head.

She sighed, but before she could resume, a new voice called a weary "Hello."

I turned to the door where Keirsten stood, hands folded in front of her, face glowing from the tiny, bursting stars inside the Chaos Machine. I looked to Dr. Aker, who was stunned, even a little afraid. I waited for someone to talk.

"What's wrong with it?" Keirsten asked me.

Again, I looked to Dr. Aker, waiting for the woman to unleash a dense, impenetrable wave of data. But she didn't she remained silent, staring at Keirsten, who in turn was staring at me.

"Um," I finally started, unable to bear the awkwardness. "I don't really know, but maybe the doctor could illuminate us?"

I looked to Dr. Aker, but she was no help. Keirsten's beautiful, right eyebrow was as arched as it could be. She was unknotting me, trying to figure me out with an intensity I didn't understand.

"Dr. Aker?" I tried again. "Help?"

I heard someone running through the tube towards us. Her maybe-boyfriend emerged, winded.

"You can't be here right now," he said to her. Keirsten

flinched slightly, startled by his voice. She didn't look away from me. "Come on, Keirsten, it's okay. Let's just get you back to your side of the ship."

That "your side of the ship" comment piqued my interest. She was being quarantined from me.

Without looking to her maybe-boyfriend, Keirsten turned and stomped away.

Dr. Aker let out a breath she'd been holding. She adjusted the stethoscope around her neck and gave a subtle shake of the head, answering a question bouncing around inside her own head.

"Has she ever done anything to anyone?" I asked Dr. Aker.

"No, not really."

"Not really?"

"It's complicated, Mr. Weinke. We need to keep you focused."

Dr. Aker turned to the Chaos Machine, motioned for the digital pad with the checklist and attempted to compose herself so we could get back to work. She spoke slower now, less assured. I wasn't sure if she was compensating for my density or still unsettled by Kiersten.

2.5

I saw Kiersten again a week later while I was in my greenhouse. I was required to tend to my plants once a day for "emotional stabilization and to reinforce nurturing instincts." I now wore my Halo more often than not, steadily working my way into the community of ghosts.

The day before, I found a singing plant in the greenhouse. It sang with a beautiful male falsetto. Nothing intelligible, but a flowing melody that almost sounded like an Italian opera. Maybe it was Italian. I should've asked Gossomer to translate. I always think of things like that way too late. With deep regret, I restarted the Chaos Machine.

Today, I hoped the plant would be back, but nope. Kiersten was though. Or rather she was three greenhouses away, visible through the greenhouses' glass walls. Another worker stood in a room between us and noticed Kiersten and I staring at one another. Feeling like I should acknowledge the moment somehow, I waved and forced a pleasant smile. Keirsten's eyes narrowed on me. The worker between us knocked on the window looking out into the hallway. A passing crew member noticed, looked to me, then to Keirsten. He ran through the Tube, returning moments later with Kiersten's maybe-boyfriend. He slipped into Kiersten's greenhouse and they argued before she finally agreed to leave for her side of the ship. Again, Kiersten refused to look away from me.

The next time I saw her was in the mess hall three days later. She emerged and stormed along the tables, crew members jumping out of her way as Kierston marched toward me. She slammed her fist on the table next to mine.

"Who are you talking to?" she growled.

I looked to the others sitting around me. They looked away from her like they were averting their gazes from a mad dog.

"Um, this is Joshua and this is Gabriel," I replied, wary, pointing from one person to the next. "And this is … ah hell, doctor something or other."

"Doctor Masterson," a quiet man with too-big glasses said, helpfully. He hadn't really been a part of our group, but I would have felt bad not including him.

"Yes, Doctor Masterson," I said, looking up to Keirsten and smiling. "Would you like to join us?"

"No!" she shouted. "Just shut the hell up for just an hour okay? You are driving me insane."

Kiersten turned her back to me, putting her hand to her forehead. The mess hall was silent and waiting. I looked for her maybe-boyfriend. I looked for Esperanza. I reached to pull off the Halo just to remove myself from this terrible moment.

"I'm sorry," she said, and I paused, leaving the Halo in place. "I'm sorry, okay. I'm just having a hard time and I don't know what is wrong with you and I am very nervous about this entire situation. I wasn't told you were going to be—"

She hugged herself, took an unsteady breath. She was not a crier. She was close to breaking down, but was fighting to hold herself together. A crew member stood up from a few tables down and ran out the door.

"It's all very weird for me too," I said, now knowing I was on my own as none of the crew were stepping up to help. "I am sorry if I upset you somehow. I didn't really know what I was getting into and had a bit of a rough time adjusting to this life. I will try to do better."

She refused to look back at me.

"Thank you," she said. "When you are in Tube 3, if you could keep your voice down. I mean, if you have to talk to get by, whatever, just keep it down. I'll stay on my side of the ship and you stay on yours and everything will be honkey dorey."

I couldn't help but chuckle at the term. It caught me off guard.

Finally, her maybe-boyfriend emerged through the door, Esperanza hurrying just behind. I decided that I didn't like her maybe-boyfriend's stupid, pretty face with his defined jawline and blue eyes. He looked fake, like he was assembled by parents too afraid to let nature decide for them. But they also forgot to add a personality. He wasn't good enough for Kiersten, I decided. He was almost at the table. I stood, pressed the button on my Halo to make it go green, then held out my hand to him.

"We haven't met." This took him back and he looked from me to Kiersten to Esperanza.

"Seth," he managed. "Human Relations Assistant Director." His ghost hand buzzed when it grasped mine. We didn't so much as shake as just squeeze like testing the ripeness of a piece of fruit.

Human Relations Assistant Director. It made sense to me and I now felt comfortably superior to him. Keirsten looked around her, then back to me, confused.

"I told you to stay in Tube 1," Seth snapped at her. Her eyes jerked away at the sound of his voice. I wanted to punch his stupid, pretty face and wondered if the Halo would let me do that.

"Seth," I announced, stepping beyond Kiersten, creating a subtle wall between them. "We're good. We just needed to discuss a few things. We are all hunkey dorey."

I savored the feel of the silly word. I decided to say it to Kiersten again at some point, to make it a thing we said that no one else said. A connection.

She followed my eyes to Seth, then looked back to me. Seth was very uncomfortable and Esperanza was on the verge of panic.

"Oh, okay," he said, glancing at Esperanza.

"Come on, Will," Esperanza said. "Leave your tray. It's time for your workout."

The moment was difficult and weird. It felt like they were bracing, trying to keep a schoolyard fight from breaking out. My tablemates were also distancing themselves, scooting down the benches with trays in hand.

"Seriously, guys," I said. "Stop acting like lunatics, her and I are good."

Kiersten was staring at me, unknotting again.

Without a better idea of what to do, I turned away from all of them and escaped the mess hall. Esperanza caught up with me as I neared the gym.

"I'm sorry about that," she said.

"It's okay, it really is. I kinda feel bad for her. Why is she still at Koi? Why not send her home?"

"It's complicated for people like us. Going home is never easy."

"You sound like a country song."

2.6

Months passed. Kiersten settled down a bit, waving back to me if we encountered each other in the greenhouses or in Tube 3. The crew members still kept us apart, Gossomer wouldn't allow me into her side of the ship, but a calm did return. I managed to say "hunkey dorey" to her, and she smiled but it didn't become a thing, sadly.

The anomalies settled a bit, appearing once a week rather than once a day. Whatever Dr. Aker was doing was working. Something to do with "cosmic harmony" and "subatomic integration". Whatever.

My favorite anomalies were now:

1. The upper torso of a goat-looking thing with spiraled horns and a sharp fangs. Terrifying. It was still alive and reached its cloven foot toward me for help. I didn't sleep well for a week.

2. A small, searing hot star in the locker room. Three metal lockers melted from its proximity.

3. A kind of shining disco box that was endlessly bouncing up and down Tube Five. It cast colors all across the walls in a nonsensical pattern.

My oldest boy told me he was planning on taking a break from college to join the Peace Corps. I was surprised that it still existed. My youngest son was living in my house over the summer and was planning on transferring to a local college to save money. I assured him money wasn't an issue, but I knew that once his mind was made, it was made.

They worried about the anomalies more than I did,

but were still proud of me. My oldest son was wearing a gold band on his ring finger that he didn't mention and I obsessed over why.

It had been nine months. A woman could have conceived and given birth in the time that I had been away from Earth.

I found a puncture in the hull. Another anomaly. No oxygen was escaping through the porthole-looking puncture, but I could clearly look out into the empty space beyond. I realized it was the first time I'd seen outside the ship since the space elevator.

I sat on the far wall, staring out of the porthole. Word traveled fast, as it always did when an anomaly appeared. Crew members assembled around the porthole and we just watched space. It wasn't like clouds outside an airplane. All the little lights were so far away that it was impossible to distinguish any movement. But it was still nice to see outside. I counted twenty stars outside the porthole. One was a little red. I thought about asking if anyone knew if it was a planet or a star. I seemed to remember Jupiter being red, but maybe that was wrong. I didn't want to ask and be wrong, so we all just watched silently, appreciating.

"I want to throw something through it," I announced. "Is that dumb?"

No one responded, but they watched me, clearly hoping that I would do it despite how dumb it might be.

"What do you guys have plenty of that we could do without here? Nothing perishable."

"A tool, like a wrench?" a guy asked. The rest of the crew members nodded in agreement. "We can just swap out when you arrive."

The plan was forming, which thrilled me. I was always

a lead-from-the-front kind of guy when it came to doing something stupid.

It was a quick hustle to the Chaos Machine room to grab one of twelve wrenches of different sizes. I should have put more thought into which wrench to throw out into space, but knew if I thought at all, I'd talk myself out of the moment.

Gossomer's speech bubbles had a lot of exclamation points, but I couldn't be bothered with his lack of adventurousness.

Back at the porthole, the crowd was dense and eager.

"Are you fucking kidding me, Will?" Esperanza asked, but I was not fucking kidding her.

I walked past, stood beside the porthole, looked across the faces, seeing Gossomer waving his arms "no" with terrified eyes. I winked at him, turned, and tossed the wrench out into the cold of space.

Space seemed to catch it, the pull of gravity easing, the bowed flight straightening and the wrench drifting away.

The crowd cheered. High fives were exchanged, with me receiving an electric version from a crew member with a green-glowing Halo. I was thrilled, the best I'd felt since breaking it off with Esperanza. I wanted to throw something else out of the porthole.

Then everything went wrong.

My body jerked off the ground. I tumbled toward the porthole, sucked toward it along with all the oxygen. The porthole seemed to be gasping, like a mouth from a reanimated dead man. My arms and legs slapped against the wall around the porthole, I struggled to push myself away from the sucking portal of death.

"Reset! Reset!"

Gossomer was clapping, panicked, trying to get his genie power working.

"Reset goddamnit!"

The crew was terrified, watching, no one moving, no one with an idea of how to help. Esperanza was screaming.

Then the sucking stopped and I fell to the ground. I scrambled away from the porthole. I could still see the wrench drifting away, at peace with its plight as space trash.

The porthole gasped again. My body flew toward it.

The suction stopped. I fell, rolled to my feet, and sprinted for the Chaos Machine.

The porthole gasped, the wind tugging at me, but I grabbed the edge of the wall and pulled myself around the corner. I worried about the oxygen reserves, about the ship pulling itself apart, about orphaning my children who would not be paid because I just had to throw a wrench out into space. I destroyed the ship and killed everyone outside Koi.

Gossomer waited for me outside the Chaos Machine, jumping up and down, cheering me on. The wind was still powerful, but I kept my feet and lunged through the door. Just like an action film, I jumped across the room and slapped the Reset button.

Lights extinguished. The hum of the engines silenced. Gossomer was gone. Only thin yellow neons were left on. The emergency lights lined the tubes, casting shadows everywhere.

I turned to the sleeping Chaos Machine, looking for the tiny big bangs, but it was only an inky black nothingness. A dead universe.

I thought of the wrench, wondering if it was the one thing that could fix the machine.

I placed my fingers on the Chaos Machine, tapping the glass, stroking it encouragingly.

"Come on, girl. You can do it. I am so sorry, I promise I won't do it again, just fire up for me, baby."

"Out of the way!" a voice shouted.

I spun, stunned. Kiersten stood before me. I didn't move. I couldn't move.

She grabbed me by the arm and yanked me from the machine. She knelt down beside it and opened a panel beneath the glass chamber. Wires spewed out.

"Hand me a number three!" she growled.

"What the hell?"

"A number three!"

She pointed toward the wall of tools. The empty space for the wrench now glared like a deep chasm. I moved to the wrenches and read over the numbers

Fortunately, the number three was still hanging in place rather than tumbling through space. I grabbed the wrench and turned to Kiersten, staring at her.

"Damnit, Will, I need your help!"

"What's happening?" I asked.

"You reset the Chaos Machine but it stalled. We have to wake it up right fucking now, so give me a number three!"

I approached, handing the wrench to her while standing as far away as I could. There was an interior panel with two bolts which she began loosening.

"Why are you real?" I asked. Stupid.

"What?" she asked.

So stupid.

I couldn't think of another way to ask the question. "Why are you real? You aren't real. I mean, somewhere you are real. Like, at Koi. You are real there, so why are you real here?"

My mother called this "kerfuffled". I was kerfuffled, down to my core. My nostrils were now aware of her smell. A skin lotion with a hint of beeswax, something floral.

"Are the others real now?" I furthered. So goddamn stupid.

Kiersten sighed, paused her work and looked back at me.

"I need you to hold it together, Will. Let's get through this moment, then you go back to your side of the ship and I'll go back to mine. We only have two more years until we get to Koi, you can do it."

I then noticed she didn't have a Halo. I Then realized that I'd never seen her with a Halo. As I said, I always notice these things too late.

I laughed. There was nothing else left to do. I laughed. I thought about poking her in the shoulder. I desperately wanted to poke her in the shoulder. It was all I could think about doing.

Until I thought about how she looked at me, talking to the crew members in the mess hall, outside my room the day they appeared and I had screamed. She never had a Halo. She didn't see what I saw.

Instead she saw an insane man talking to air.

"I didn't know you were on board," I said finally.

She focused on her work, pulling out the inner panel. She plucked a penlight from her pocket and looked inside.

"I thought you were another projection," I said. "This entire time. I had no idea you were real."

"Well, now you do, so help me please. There should be wire cutters on the wall. Grab them please. Where is the number six wrench?"

I walked to the wall, found the clippers, then looked to the blank space where my space wrench should have been.

"Do we really need the number six?" I asked.

"I don't know, maybe. Where is it?"

I shrugged. I couldn't tell her I threw it out a porthole and it was now gone forever.

"Maybe they forgot to pack it?"

Kiersten chewed her lip, took a breath, then motioned for the wire cutters. I obliged, feeling her fingertips brush against my palm. It was the most amazing thing. The room was feeling small and I wanted to step outside and catch my breath. Settle myself.

But I stayed to help.

"Do you have a Halo?" I asked.

Kiersten slammed down the wire cutters and glared back at me.

"I can't do this right now, Will. I need you to stop being weird for just a few more minutes."

"No, I mean this," I said, pulling off my Halo and showing it to her. "This is a Halo. They gave me one and I was just wondering if you have one too."

She took the Halo, looked it over, examining the lights on the end, now dark. She handed it back to me.

"No."

I took in a deep breath, then chuckled.

"Okay, this all makes sense now. You thought I was talking to myself this whole time. It's the Halo. I talk to the crew members from the ship by Koi. I'm not crazy. I swear. And you, I thought you were one of them. They didn't tell me you were on this ship, so, Jesus, what you must have thought of me."

She was studying me now. She looked back to the Halo.

"So what do you see now?" she asked. "If you put it back on?"

"Nothing, it is tied to the Chaos Machine."

She didn't believe me, not entirely. She turned back to the panel and started clipping wires. Like this we worked for almost an hour, her calling out for wire, for drill bits, for electrical tape, for a multimeter, but not discussing this amazing thing that just happened. This amazing thing that'd been happening for nine months.

I was living with the most beautiful woman I'd ever seen, but I had no idea that she was real and she had no idea that I wasn't bonkers.

Story of my life.

***

A blue flair sent sparks bouncing around the glass inside the Chaos Machine. Swirls of reds and oranges. White tracers bounding off in random directions. Then darkness. Another blue flair. Another. And another. Tiny stars began forming. Lights in the tubes flickered, fighting for life. The hum of the engine announced itself. The gentle buzz of my Halo.

Kiersten sat away from the Chaos Machine, the panel still open, wires splayed out like intestines. She pulled her hair away from her face and wiped the sweat away.

"I thought if the Chaos Machine went down, we would turn back for home automatically," I said. "But the engines stopped when it stopped."

Kiersten glanced back at me, a half-grin on her face.

"There is no turning back for us, Will," she said, and I believed her in a way that frightened and exhilarated me.

She held out her hand to me, wanting help to stand up. I clasped her palm, tugging her to her feet. She was close to me. I'd forgotten what a human felt like, just the air around them, the way it stirred. I was still humiliated that I hadn't sorted it out before now.

"Let's get something to eat and then come back to finish this up," she suggested and I agreed, just wanting to be near her.

She looked up to my Halo, looking at the blue lights.

"What do you see now?" she asked.

"Just you."

We emerged to find crew members surrounding the room. I paused and Kiersten turned to look at me. She couldn't see what I could see.

"Everything is working," I announced. "And you guys are dicks. Each and every one of you."

Kiersten grinned. I removed the Halo and the crew members evaporated. I held out the Halo to Kiersten and she hesitated. She met my eyes, that beautifully arched eyebrow. She took it, slipped it over her head, the blue lights glowed. She gazed across the tube, seeing what I could not.

She laughed. She laughed and laughed and laughed. It was the most beautiful sound I'd ever heard, like a million bouncy balls falling onto a highway during rush hour.

PART 3

Kiersten jumped on the bed and tried to squeeze off my nipples. She did this often. I couldn't stop laughing and was forced to kick her away while hiding under the covers like a bullied child.

When this began between us, not too long after the Chaos Machine went down, we met incognito in the middle of the night. Gossomer followed close behind as we crept back to my private chamber. He scowled which made the moment even more fun, just like back in high school, sneaking kisses in closed bedrooms before the parents got home from work.

As time passed and rumors were confirmed, Dr. Hagin lectured me on the chaos that would result if this thing between Kiersten and I went sideways.

"But chaos is what keeps the ship alive," I said, so thrilled with myself that I couldn't stop smiling the rest of the day.

Our overlords finally yielded and prepared for the worst. Yet, the worst never entered my own mind. I never feared what we had, convinced that this velvet sun casting its mesmerizing glow down upon us would always shine. I didn't think of the end. I could not think of it because of the spell of love. It muted all but happiness.

But there was this:

"One year and 212 more days on this ship," she whispered, her leg wrapped over my hips, her head on my shoulder, her right hand gently picking at the gray strands of my chest hair. I knew, if she were in a better mood, she would pluck a hair out just to see how I would react. Not when she was sad, though.

"Then 183 days above Koi, then you are gone forever."

There was nothing to say. Our brilliant story had a fixed end point. She would stay to replace a deceased engineer, I would go home to my children and my new-found wealth. The money was nothing to me now because it would not replace her. I would stay if I could, but I couldn't leave my boys behind and I couldn't ask her to give up on her dream to be a space explorer. She'd wanted to step on alien soil since she was a child, and, in one year and 212 days, she would be within the orbit of a new planet. Within five years, she would be part of the first exploratory mission to the planet's surface.

A life fulfilled. I could not take that from her. I could not, so I simply didn't think about the then. I thought only of the now, how her waist was shaped perfectly for my hands. How, when I picked her up, her thighs squeezed against me and refused to let me put her back down. Not that I ever wanted to. I would carry her forever, if not in my arms, then in my heart.

Of the seven nights that came in a week, at least two ended in this heavy, sad fog.

A million bouncy balls can't bounce forever. She needed her time of rest. I couldn't help with the storms in her mind, I could only hold on, listen, and anchor her so the waves didn't sweep her away.

Perhaps I even loved her more at these moments because this was when she seemed the strongest.

I now understood and felt the vastness of space, for soon it would separate us.

3.2

The anomalies stopped the day they almost sucked me out into the vacuum of space. The day that Kiersten and I truly met. Not one of the crew members could make any sense of the cause of the anomalies nor the cause of their absence.

"Maybe because the reset took so long?" Dr. Aker asked Dr. Hagin as she looked to the handful of other scientists crammed into the Chaos Machine room. Just because they were just projections did not diminish the claustrophobia. Every time a projection accidentally swept into me, it made me want to vomit. Every time.

No answers came. Kiersten's fingers laced inside mine, but her eyes were still fixed on the Chaos Machine. She did that often, while deep in thought, reach out to me. I couldn't tell if she was reminding me that she was there or reminding herself that I was. It didn't matter, I still liked it.

"Isn't it a good thing, no matter why the anomalies stopped?" I asked, feeling very obtuse as to why everyone was so worried. A leaky faucet that no longer dripped was no longer a leaky faucet.

"Eventually this will take us across the universe, darling," Kiersten said and I resented the addition of "darling." I hated what it implied to the others. If I was younger, I would have replied with something shitty just to make a point, but I was old and highly skilled at picking my battles.

"Right, so we'd prefer a fully functioning Chaos Machine not coughing up beating hearts and animated jelly beans, right?" I asked.

"Yes, of course," Kiersten replied. "But there is a factor

that stopped the anomalies and we need to understand what that factor is in case it will have disastrous consequences down the road."

"Like a muffler that stops rattling right before falling off entirely?" I asked.

"Exactly," Kiersten said, smirking at me.

We all watched the Chaos Machine in a curious awe. I wanted the Chaos Machine to speak, just all of a sudden like it was no big deal. Living in a Community Pod allowed me to recover the childish assumption that all things were possible. Nothing was beyond reality now. I could go to sleep a white man and wake up an orange. It was just a matter of likelihood.

"We've sent all the data back to X-Verse," Dr. Aker began with that sharp tone that indicated one of her information hurricanes just made landfall. Kiersten squeezed my hand in recognition. "They are going analyze every anomaly, every second of every day since the Chaos Machine went live, look for patterns, look for any possible cause and effect. In the meantime, we are going to retrace wiring, connections, coding, eliminate as many variables as we can."

And like this it went. My father spoke like Dr. Aker when he was lecturing me, a technique he picked up from his father, exhausting teenage rebellion through endless talk. He'd corner me in my room after I snuck back into the house. He'd rolled from bed, only wearing socks and underwear, then proceeded to talk about responsibilities and the dangers of the world after midnight. I'd be asked about how my actions impacted my mother, how they would impact my grades at school and, later, my jobs and girlfriends and wives and children.

He was torturing me and it worked. I'd take a leather belt over his lectures, which he knew and relished. It kept me on the straight and narrow, just to avoid answering for my actions.

Crew members began shuffling out of the room. A call to action had happened and I missed it. I stood still, waiting for Kiersten to lead me forward, translate the technical jargon and lay out my mission in terms simple enough for a child.

I often felt unworthy of her, but she insisted that I was smart in my own way. Like a dopey dog galloping through the mud that she loved all the more for my simplicity.

***

We squeezed into the guts of the Community Pod, laying shoulder to shoulder on our backs, wiggling along with headlamps illuminating the bands of wires stretching underneath the floors. Kiersten felt the wires, twisting the groups around, looking for wear, burn marks, anything to indicate a problem.

"I know this will make me sound like a moron," I began. "But the anomalies stopped when we started. Maybe that's the factor."

Kiersten released the wire and sighed, not it didn't sound like exasperated because what I said was moronic, but maybe because she thought the same thing and also felt like a moron for thinking it.

"That makes no sense, Will. The Chaos Machine doesn't give a shit about us fucking."

I loved it when she said "fucking". Sharp and visceral, as sexy as sexy ever gets. I'd have kissed her if I had enough room to roll over on my side. The fact that I couldn't made me even hungrier.

"Are you sure?" I asked. "I don't know about you, but I was struggling alone. I made due the best I could, but I was lonely, I was bored, I was a little frustrated. The things I made poor Gossomer do."

Kiersten chuckled. I still tormented the furry, little guy, often sending him with messages to Kiersten wearing tu-tus or beer hats or his hair shaved into "I" heartshape "K". If a computer program was capable of hate, then Gossomer's hate would be heavier than the ship and burn hotter than the suns inside the Chaos Machine.

"I was lonely too," Kiersten said. "I was pretty miserable, but you are assuming the Chaos Machine has the ability to care about us, which it doesn't. It doesn't feel, it doesn't coddle to us, it doesn't react to us, it's just chaos."

"Are you willing to bet your life on that assumption?"

Kiersten didn't answer, but kept her headlamp pointed above. We listened to each other breath for several moments before she returned her fingers to the wire. We wriggled further through the shaft.

"Anything is possible," I said. "With everything we have seen, it is clear that the Chaos Machine is capable of way more than we can understand, so maybe it is capable of reacting to us. It isn't just exploding stars, it is creation. We try to tame it, try to guide it, but maybe it is trying to guide us too."

"You are saying the chaos is intelligent," she said, still examining the wires.

"Maybe it is."

We wriggled more, the space cramping more and more, but comforting me by how private it felt. I couldn't share these thoughts with anyone else on the ship because I knew I would be laughed at. With Kiersten, if I was wrong, she would tell me and patiently explain where my logic went awry.

I was waiting for her to explain, but she only seemed to be poking at my idea in her mind, turning it over to examine it from all angles, looking for the flaw, the loose string that would untangle it all.

"How would we test your theory?" she asked.

I was surprised, having not considered my idea getting this far.

"By arguing?" she asked. "We change the atmosphere on the ship, break up, prod the Chaos Machine to react?"

She said all this with a hint of anger, maybe feeling helpless to the confusion of quantum mechanics, or maybe feeling helpless to the weight of sorrow that would fall on us when I turned for Earth, never to see her again. It was hard to tell, so I only answered the question.

"I don't think I could survive the lose of a single day with you."

The words felt funny, overly formal, but the moment felt significant. It felt like something was suddenly defined. A telescope aimed at a distant miracle, finally finding its focus.

At that moment, I was certain that we would be in harmony forever.

And, of course, I was wrong.

3.3

I was old enough to know how it worked. You start off bonded by this tangled mess of emotional taffy, with every motion away, you are tugged back. Rich, sweet, it feels endless and perfect.

But then we drift and that taffy turns into airy strings, still tethering us, still yanking our heartstrings when we get a bit too far away.

The taffy dissolves slowly, the solvent being subtle discord that was once hidden beneath the sea of love, but surface as the tide retreats

The taffy fades to just threads of smoke, tumbling, breaking, reforming. Eventually finding only emptiness. She drifted too far away.

I know how this works. I know not to swim out for her because she will drown us both. I know how this works.

The last night for us, she crept into my bed and curled against me. I awoke in stages, first startled, then pulling her head onto my chest, then turning toward her, then long and savoring kisses, knowing that they might be the last tastes I have of her.

Time. It destroyed us. The time we had. The time we wouldn't have. Less than a year left including our six months at Koi. Her heart was throwing up shelter, preparing for the pain. I was doing the same, which is why I was letting her go.

She once kept track of our remaining time together, announcing it every night before we slipped into sleep. But not tonight. The clock was too heavy to hold anymore.

She woke before me, left before I said "goodbye." She

retreated to the far side of the Community Pod. We ended without one real fight in all the time we spent together. Maybe because there was nothing to fight about. I had to return home to my family, she had to seek out her destiny. Arguments would not solve the impossibility, it would only make us hate each other.

The days crept onward. I hoped to see her, perhaps through the greenhouses or in the mess hall, even if she sat several tables away.

My Halo rarely left the side table now. I forced Gossomer to make the walls white again. I could not take sensory, I could not suffer company or solace. I only wanted to marinate in the pain. It was my way. I knew how I worked.

3.4

Shuffling brought my attention away from my modest little rose bush. My heart stirred at the thought that Kiersten could be coming back to me for a last burst of passion before we parted forever. But then I remembered the pain and the heart retreated back inside its hard shell.

I turned back to the roses, admiring their vibrant, fleshy petals. Growing flowers in space seemed a dumb thing to do, but Gossomer insisted, saying that they fed the heart while the green beans fed the body. My greenhouse was flush with life now, after almost three years of work. My thumb had turned a few shades more green, the plants standing in passably for the dogs and children I'd once doted on. I call them by their names Professor Wigglebutt, Senior Hotsauce, or Reginald Stickinthemud III. These were the names Kiersten gave them. She named everything, from her pet spoon (Woodsworth Spoondoggle) to the robot spider monkeys (Pete, Skip, and Skadoodle).

But the roses were new and grew in her absence. I named them all after former loves, my ex-wife standing tall near the back, The rose named Kiersten was tucked near the front, looking up through the taller flowers with brash defiance. I knew the greenhouse would be mine for only a few more days as the Community Pod approached the jump site.

I often thought of how the crew members would treat me once I arrived and how they would treat Kiersten. We broke the rules. We fell in love. Would they be angry? Would we be punished? Would we all just act weird until I finally fled back out into the stars?

The shuffling again.

I turned from my plants and walked toward the window, looking out to see who was outside my greenhouse. No Kiersten. I chalked it up to imagination, removed my gloves, and opened the door to the greenhouse.

I staggered my meals so that the mess hall would be mostly empty by the time I arrived. Even if I couldn't see the crew members, I didn't like the idea of sitting amid dozens of them while I ate, all of them whispering back and forth, shaking their heads, saying horrible things like "what did he expect to happen?"

I could also take my meals in my room, but that seemed a bit too pathetic and cowardly.

The door to the mess hall hissed open.

Two giant green eyes looked back at me.

I screamed and fell backwards, scrambling away. The door slid closed before I had an idea of what I'd seen.

"Gossomer!" I shouted.

He appeared, eyebrow arched in confused worry.

"What the hell was that?" I asked, pointing at the mess hall door.

Gossomer looked back to the door, then turned to me with a shrug.

"Inside damnit!"

Gossomer rolled his eyes, disappeared. In a few moments he reappeared, flapping his hands in panic, sort of running in place.

"Reset the Chaos Machine!" I said.

Gossomer put a paw to his head, thinking with "...." in the word bubble. He stomped his foot. "I can't seem to get the Chaos Machine to respond."

A far door leading to the mess hall opened. A lean, long-haired head with a massive, flat nose and green eyes the size of cereal bowls looked out. It stared at me. It looked like a human/giraffe mutation with an impossibly long neck arching out of the mess hall as it spied me. It eased out of the mess hall, revealing a long-limbed body with a patch of fine brown fur and a white toga. A gleaming purple brooch was fastened at the shoulder. It's knees bent the opposite direction and seemed to stand eight feet tall, having to bow slightly to keep its head off the ceiling.

"Gramble," it called timidly.

"Reset the Chaos Machine, Gossomer!"

Gossomer appeared between us and the creature startled.

"I can't," Gossomer's bubble read. "You will have to do it manually."

The door to the Chaos Machine was on the other side of the creature, of course.

"Tell Kiersten to stay out of Tube Three," I told Gossomer. "I am calling in the reinforcements."

I sprinted away from the creature back towards Tube One to retrieve my Halo.

***

The beast sat against the wall, tired, sad, and confused. The entire crew circled the beast. It did not know they watched him

I cleared my throat and he looked up to meet my eyes. He was frightened, but a smile as crooked as a dirt road emerged, hopeful. He coughed a few times, struggled to swallow the phlegm, then pushed heavily off the wall to get to his feet. I thought of gravity, how it would be affecting him if his home world was different than ours.

It would almost have to be. That our gravities were even close enough for him to walk was amazing.

I found Esperanza in the crowd.

"Has anyone talked to Kiersten yet?" I asked.

"Freaked the fuck out, Will," another voice emerged. Kiersten stepped through the crew members, their images fading slightly as she invaded their space. She was ten feet beyond the beast. He looked back to her.

"Foary lovak arb row," the beast added.

"Any chance Gossomer can translate for us?"

Gossomer appeared, shrugging. The creature examined Gossomer, leaning close, then reaching slowly for the digital projection. Gossomer retreated slightly.

"Let him," I told Gossomer.

The creature's fingers, knobby and longer than my entire hand, reached through the projection. Gossomer giggled and held his belly as if he was tickled.

"Por eil zack," the creature said with a half grin. He looked to me and bowed his head, as if congratulating me on my cleverness.

"He's intelligent," Esperanza said. "He doesn't see magic, he see's science. Wherever he came from, they have technology."

"I love him," Kiersten announced. "We are going to call him Fred Oppenheimer and assign him to the optic development lab immediately."

The crew members laughed. Kiersten caught my eye with a smile that sucked the wind from my chest and almost knocked me over.

"Of course," Dr. Hagin began. "You must reset the Chaos Machine."

"We will do no such thing, will we Dr. Fred Oppenheimer?" Kiersten said, a bit of a coo to her voice.

The creature was amused and puzzled. His long, giraffe neck swayed back so he could look to me for answers.

"Agreed, let's get the distinguished doctor some food, shall we?" I said, then motioning the creature forward to follow me back into the mess hall.

"But Will!" Dr. Hagin began, but I removed my Halo.

The creature lumbered forward, skeptical, but clearly desperate for some hope to cling to. He coughed, then followed with a smile. It reminded me of a terrible car wreck I'd had. Blood had sprayed out of my scalp in 4/4 time, I couldn't focus my right eye, and all I could think to do was to make friends with every nurse and doctor I came across as if charm would get them to work a bit faster.

***

Kiersten and I decided that the distinguished Dr. Fred Oppenheimer was a family practitioner who once considered research during his schooling years. He smelled vaguely of pine chips because that is what their floors were made of, which was much more comfortable to their cloven feet than carpet. At the time the Chaos Machine plucked him from his planet, he was before the board of medicine defending his decision to save the life of an impoverished child despite the family's inability to pay, so was going to lose his practice in the noblest of ways.

He was better off with us, was the purpose of the story.

Dr. Fred Oppenheimer politely refused all meats, but was a particular fan of kale and arugula. Though I suspected he had a massive appetite, he ate sparingly and waved away multiple offers of seconds. He sat awkwardly on the top of a table, his feet touching the floor. He hunched over like he was inside a child's clubhouse. His coughing was intermittent and Kiersten worried that he'd caught a bug that we had carried from Earth. I assured her that the bug wouldn't have lasted this long without a host. She still fretted.

But we were talking again. Kiersten's fingers laced in mine whenever we were close and it felt wonderful.

Gossomer appeared from time to time, insisting that we separate from the creature to discuss matters with Dr. Hagin, but we ignored the pleas no matter how many exclamation points were affixed the end of his word bubble.

Dr. Fred Oppenheimer found Gossomer fascinating and asked us to pronounce everything that appeared in the word bubbles.

"Stop. Being. An. Asshole. Will," Dr. Fred Oppenheimer repeated in a slow, slurred accent, then smiling. "Asshole."

Curse words were always the most fun.

3.5

Of course we were going to reset the Chaos Machine. I suspected Kiersten knew that too, but loneliness makes a person crazy. Bad ideas become good ideas so as long as it mutes the hollow howls of our aching hearts.

Dr. Fred Oppenheimer brought us back together, a sort of neutral ground above the poisoned marches of our past. Pain had infected every inch of the Community Pod. It would take something big to wash the pain away, so the Chaos Machine sent us an alien.

Dr. Hagin's demands to hit the reset button eased as curiosity took over. We spent the afternoon taking Dr. Fred Oppenheimer's vitals, measuring his limbs, taking a small sample of his fur. Kiersten spent a long time listening to his chest, trying to discern what was happening to his lungs to force the cough. I suggested it was simply a difference in air quality and she seemed pleased with my cleverness. I then reassured her that the cough was stable, his body just needed time to adjust, so we shouldn't worry unless it got worse.

I allowed Kiersten to take a vial of blood from me to show Dr. Fred Oppenheimer what a needle did. He smiled in the same patient way my father smiled when I asked him if he'd ever heard of The Rolling Stones.

While the nerds at Koi poured over the data and dethreaded Dr. Fred Oppenheimer's DNA, Kiersten and I cleared out room in the cargo bay to make a bed for the creature. Once he saw what we were doing, he insisted on helping. He asked for a "pillow" and a "blanket" without us having to teach him, just him picking up words from our conversation.

"I wonder if he was a linguist?" I asked. "I couldn't learn a language this fast."

We decided that Dr. Fred Oppenheimer was a professor of obscure, tribal languages and was leading an expedition through a dark continent full of exotic and terrifying monsters in a search for a cure for a plague striking his people. The rest of the expedition was devoured by a land whale with fangs the size of basketball poles, but Dr. Fred Oppenheimer was plucked from certain death by the Chaos Machine.

I suspected Dr. Fred Oppenheimer had a family. His timid nature exuded fatherly patience. He was likely a religious man too.

Someone missed him greatly. These thoughts ripped into my heart. I felt an urge to tell Kiersten that we needed to reset the Chaos Machine in hope that it would send Dr. Fred Oppenheimer back home, but I feared losing her for these final days we had left before the jump.

***

We decided, for safety's sake, that we should sleep in the same bed. I couldn't hold her tight enough.

3.6

A meeting was called for the entire crew to discuss the fate of Dr. Fred Oppenheimer. We installed the creature in front of a screen so that he could continue absorbing our language.

"We will need some answers from him," Dr. Hagin announced.

"About?" Kiersten asked.

We looked across the dozens of faces that I'd become accustomed to. I would be seeing these faces in their true flesh soon. They are the lives that I have helped save. I would be giving them the greatest love of my life, depositing her on their ship, then floating away.

I was trying to keep the hurt at bay, but it intruded at unexpected moments. Kiersten seemed to sense it and leaned against me.

"Analysis of his fur and skin, his bone density, and his lungs prove that this is a habitable world," Dr. Hagin said. "We are trying to go through the records of the Chaos Machine to find any kind of hint of where it found him, but that could take decades. We need to see if he can tell us himself."

"So, we aren't going to reset the machine after all," Dr. Aker asked.

"No, we cannot afford to lose the creature."

"Dr. Fred Oppenheimer," Kiersten snapped.

Dr. Hagin frowned. Kiersten arched her eyebrow in a clear warning. She didn't appreciate the creature being treated like a creature. When she loved, she loved quickly and as fierce as a mother bear.

"We need to find his planet," Dr. Hagin said. "Many of you know that Koi is quickly revealing itself as a dead end. If we can find out where he came from, we can move our facilities there and begin laying the groundwork for a colony."

Kiersten's fingers tightened around mine, squeezing out rage.

"No one told me that Koi was a dead end," Kiersten said.

"Dead end is a poor choice of words," Dr. Aker cut in. "We still have hope that we can find habitable solutions, but the lands could take generations to develop before they could sustain human life. But the planet of Mr. Oppenheimer —"

"Dr. Oppenheimer," Kiersten said.

"Yes, sorry, Dr. Oppenheimer. His world could allow us immediate opportunities for colonization. We could begin studying their plant life, looking for fresh water, analyzing their air quality. The gravity difference will be a little problematic, but we could adapt. We must pursue it. It is the best opportunity we've had since we began deep space exploration."

Voices were rising, chatter, whispers, excitement and skepticism.

"I don't like it," Kiersten whispered to me.

I nodded in agreement, but also knew that we didn't have much choice.

"What we also know is that we cannot risk waiting for Dr. Fred Oppenheimer to reach Koi," Dr. Hagin continued. "He may not make it. The jump could reset him back to where he came from or potentially zap him out of existence. We need to find out about his planet, his star, his solar system. We need clues to look for so we can track down his home planet."

"We also need to get him home," Dr. Akin added.

"Yes," Hagin said. "Kiersten and Will, do you think you are up for it?"

All faces turned toward us. I could sense Kiersten's hesitation. I stood.

"Of course you can count on us," I began. "But we aren't going to hurt him. He will tell us what he will tell us."

Kiersten smiled at this.

"Of course," Dr. Hagin said. "We aren't the military. We are X-Verse."

I didn't find the distinction comforting.

***

"Ha-llow," Dr. Fred Oppenheimer said with an elegant wave of his hand. He stood up from the severely undersized chair, straightened as much as the ceiling would allow, and stretched his back. He coughed.

Dr. Hagin followed us into the room as I carried a small data pad.

"Good evening, how are you feeling?" Kiersten asked, her bright, motherly smile glowing.

Dr. Fred Oppenheimer's big green eyes glanced away as he searched her words, trying to recall their meaning and cobble together a response. He looked to us with a wide smile.

"Hurt," he replied, then pointed up. I couldn't imagine how sore his neck must be.

"I bet," Kiersten said, then waving for him to follow. "Come with us, we will get you back to your bed so you can lay down."

He hobbled behind us as we wove our way back to the loading bay. He rolled down heavily onto his bedding and stretched out as much as he could. His long fingers massaged the vertebrae in his neck, working out kinks. I thought about offering a massage, but there were just too many weird implications involved.

"Show him," Dr. Hagin instructed me. Since Dr. Fred Oppenheimer didn't have a Halo, I had to be Dr. Hagin's ventriloquist's puppet.

I lifted up the data pad, facing it toward him. He rolled his head towards it, looking over a series of stars of different colors.

"Stars," I said. I then pointed to a yellow orb. "Our star. We call it the 'sun'."

He gazed at the star with a curious smile.

"Which is yours?" I asked. Kiersten breathed a deep sigh. I met her eyes and smiled. Dr. Fred Oppenheimer caught the exchange and then settled on my face.

"No," he said.

"No?" Dr. Hagin asked. "What does he mean?"

"What do you mean? Do you not have a star?"

Dr. Fred Oppenheimer pushed up onto an elbow, his head raising to meet mine at eye level.

"You find star, you find us."

The words chilled me.

"Three things happen," he continued. He held up one of his four long fingers. "You. Science." He held up two fingers. "Others. Money." He held up his third finger. "Last. Boom."

"Scientists, then traders, than conquerors," Kiersten said

to Dr. Hagin. "I told you he was smart."

Dr. Hagin frowned.

"Tell him that we understand, but would like him to know more about who we are as a people," Dr. Hagin said. "Maybe that will change his mind."

"He won't change his mind because he is right," Kiersten said, looking at Dr. Hagin. I followed her eyes, then saw Dr. Fred Oppenheimer watching us curiously. To him, Kiersten was talking into blank space. I wondered if he'd already sorted it out or just thought we were a bit bonkers.

"Still, let's try," Dr. Hagin said.

"Okay," I shrugged, turning the data pad to face me. "What do you want me to pull up for him?"

"The discovery of the New World."

"The New World as in America?" I asked.

"Yes."

"We can't just skip over what happened to the Native Americans," Kiersten said.

"Of course we can't," Dr. Hagin said. "That's the most important part. And have him brush up on his English too. I would like to talk to him myself."

3.7

We whittled away the final days before our jump sitting with Dr. Fred Oppenheimer. He was capable of telling us his name, but we had yet to ask. He seemed content to instead carry on with Kiersten's moniker. Perhaps the anonymity made him feel safer.

He never spoke of his home world, his family, his beliefs, only listened with those kind and bright green eyes. I'd lost my fear of his size and exoticness, but his intelligence troubled and intimidated me.

Though he rarely spoke, he absorbed everything, sitting cross-legged in his makeshift chamber that looked a little like a Turkish opium den. We'd pulled in a large monitor and it played videos on American history, the Native American genocide, the slave trade, the Vietnam War, the Civil Rights struggle, European Colonialism, the Holocaust. I was horrified and confused.

As we ate in the mess hall together, Dr. Fred Oppenheimer asked us questions about our life, never mentioning the vast cruelty our species was capable of.

"Yes, two boys," I told him. He smiled. "Well, men. I still call them boys though they are much bigger and wiser than myself."

"Tell me about them," Dr. Fred Oppenheimer said.

"They're better than I deserve. Strong, kind, weird. I stayed home with them when they were young, letting my then-wife go off to start her career. I always wanted to be close to them. The joke was that our kids were like cactus, we just had to add water from time to time, which was true. We spent so much time playing, making silly short movies, talking about life, arguing about superheroes. We were three tight-knit eccentrics and their personalities branched out in these beautiful ways as they got older. We were all obsessive about something, bull-headed, and would talk forever. As they reached their teenage years, that connection got a little strained, as I guess it's supposed to. The divorce happened and they weathered it, but I felt myself becoming more desperate for their attention. I was poor, barely holding the house together, but thought that if I could still be that dad that they always talked to, that they connected with, then it would be okay that I could barely scrape together the money for groceries while my house was falling apart. I wanted them to be proud of me, but I could tell they were beginning to see me for what I really was."

"And what is that, Will?" he asked.

"A man worth leaving behind."

His large hand covered mine, his rectangular teeth emerging with his kind smile. Kiersten inched closer to me, laying her head on my shoulder. I felt pathetic for how badly I needed this moment to last.

"And you can still talk to them from inside this ship?" Dr. Fred Oppenheimer asked.

"Yes, there is long delay, so we send each other messages," I said.

"And what is it like? You've been out here how long?"

"Almost three years. We aren't what we once were, but they are adults now. They aren't mine anymore, they belong to themselves. I try not to lean on them because that isn't fair. It isn't their job to care for their sad, old pop. My parents didn't do it to me, so I shouldn't do it to them."

"He's never told me any of this," Kiersten said to Dr. Fred Oppenheimer. "You must be some sort of mental wizard."

"I've always been told that I am easy to talk to," he said,

then looking back to me. "When we travel across the universe to join with the others, you will take the other ship home to rejoin your boys?"

"Yes," I said.

Kiersten's arm laced inside of mine and she squeezed tightly against me. He looked to her.

"And you will stay behind?"

"Yes," she said.

"How very sad. Love is a very big thing to abandon."

"It is," I said as Kiersten clung to me.

A gentle silence ensued while we finished our meals and went back to watch the horrors of mankind.

***

While watching the history of the Australian aborigine, Dr. Fred Oppenheimer shifted on his bed, coughed up phlegm, then forced himself to his feet and walked to the screen. He was moving slower and slower. Perhaps it was the difference in gravity or his nagging cough was wearing on him. Either way, every movement was a struggle, but his mood remained buoyant.

His long fingers wrapped around the screen to find the power button on the back. The screen went blank. He turned to us.

"I have seen enough," he announced. "We should talk about what you plan on doing with me."

***

We met Dr. Hagin at the Chaos Machine. Kiersten and I stood inside the darkened room while Dr. Fred Oppenheimer sat outside, his long neck craning in through the door. It was his first time to see the machine and he took in its wonder passively, like a shrewd audience member looking for the mirrors at a magic show.

"Can you hear me Dr. Oppenheimer?" Dr. Hagin called.

"Yes," he responded, nodding his head, his long stringy hair waving. He often reminded me of a horse.

"Good, I am glad that we can finally talk directly," Dr. Hagin said, standing formally next to the Chaos Machine, very poised and professional though the creature could not see him.

"Yes, I've heard much about you and am anxious to hear what you have to say for yourself."

The tone was surprisingly sharp and confrontational.

"I have spent much time thinking about your refusal to tell us anything about your planet and have determined that you are very wise to be cautious with us," Dr. Hagin said. "I'd considered making the case that we are a peaceful people, but that would be a lie. We have been slave-traders, brutal colonizers, war-mongers, and genocidal conquerors."

"This seems to be a threat," Dr. Fred Oppenheimer said. His eyes narrow and steady, but still controlled.

"Not a threat, doctor. Just an admittal that we have our blights. You are an intelligent being, doctor, and you would see through my lie. You are correct that the general course of things is to send the scientists first, then the traders, then the military. Contact, form financial bonds, then colonize. That is how we do things. You are wise to shield your planet from us. Perhaps we are not the only alien race you've encountered."

Dr. Hagin waited for him to respond, but Dr. Fred

Oppenheimer would not be goaded into giving away any more information.

"Before we move forward, are you comfortable with the name we've given you or would you prefer me to call you something else?" Dr. Hagin asked.

"I am used to Oppenheimer, it suits me."

"Okay, Dr. Oppenheimer. I am going to now make my case why you should reconsider. In twelve hours, the glowing machine before you will jump this ship across the universe. It will be instantaneous. You may jump with the ship or you may go back to your home planet or you may disappear into nothingness. We have no control of it, the Chaos Machine will do what it chooses to do."

"Your own god in a bottle," Dr. Fred Oppenheimer said.

Dr. Hagin chuckled and looked over to us.

"Yes, I've never thought of it that way, but yes, the Chaos Machine is like having a god in a bottle. I hope that you will be returned to your planet before our environment does more damage to your body. If you make the trip with us, we might see what we can do to better accommodate you."

"Thank you."

"My pleasure. Now, I need you to understand that, with very little expended energy, we can jump to any point in this universe in moments. If we can see it, we can reach it. That is the slogan of our company. If we get an indication that a distant planet is habitable or contains resources we crave, we send out an exploration team. As we speak, our researchers are pouring over all your physical traits to estimate what sort of planet you came from. They are good at what they do and, eventually, we will find your home world. Your people will meet us one day, Dr. Oppenheimer, so what I hope to do in the next twelve hours is lay down the perimeters of how we will meet and what sort of relationship we will establish."

Dr. Fred Oppenheimer did not respond, but his eyes moved from Dr. Hagin to us. We had no answer for him. His eyes fell to the floor. Without looking back up, he spoke.

"These things you've shown me of your culture, you wanted me to see the worst of who you were to gain my trust?"

"Correct," Dr. Hagin answered. "I believe my people's treatment of the Native Americans is the most informative of our current situation. I believe that your people are more advanced, that you have high technology, perhaps a strong military, universities, functioning government. You are a people capable of diplomacy and, probably, very interested in trade."

"What makes you think that you have anything that we might value?" Dr. Fred Oppenheimer asked, meeting Dr. Hagin in the eyes.

"Because you are an intelligent, curious race, just as we are. We are going to find you, doctor, I will promise you that. Our planet's atmosphere is shifting and, within a few generations, it will become a difficult place for us to survive. That is why we are searching the universe. We made mistakes with our environment, mistakes that we are trying to correct. Some of us will survive, some of us will not, so we are searching for answers on how to live more sustainably. I suspect you have some of those answers, so we are going to find your people and get those answers however we can. This is about the survival of our race. With desperation comes opportunity, Dr. Fred Oppenheimer. If you help us, we will help you."

"And how do we keep from being like your Native Americans?"

"By controlling the terms early," Dr. Hagin answered. "By knowing who we are as a people, for our good and for our bad, and helping us dictate how we will interact. We have not weaponized the Chaos Machine or the Community Pods. But we will. Ally yourself with us early so that, when that time comes, X-Verse will stand with you instead of against you."

Dr. Fred Oppenheimer sighed. His head waved side to side, deeply troubled.

"We have been visited before," Dr. Fred Oppenheimer said. "We have battled those from other worlds. We won, but it was costly. Those visitors may one day visit you and, when they do, it will be just as devastating. They do not have anything like the Chaos Machine and they must not. I am not comfortable that you possess such a powerful thing, but you do. Our people are flawed in their own ways too, we are more alike than I prefer to admit. Thank you for showing me what you did. It was a wise move."

"So you will help us?" Dr. Hagin asked.

"Yes. We cannot survive another interstellar war, Dr. Hagin. We can be strong allies, but know that we can also find you. I believe it is called 'peace through mutually assured destruction'."

"It is."

3.8

The doctors adjourned to a lab to study star maps in an effort to pinpoint Oppenheimer's home planet. I hoped to find out his real name before the jump.

Kiersten and I carried in pillows for Dr. Fred Oppenheimer. He quickly excused us. We returned to the Chaos Machine. I pulled Kiersten into my arms and we watched the tiny exploding stars, the black holes, the clusters, the supernovas. All the space inbetween.

"A god in a bottle," Kiersten whispered.

I said nothing, instead kissing her on the head and squeezing her tight. I was close to losing her. We jump together, then six months at Koi. Then I jump again, alone.

Maybe not even six months at Koi. Dr. Hagin was anxious to jump to Dr. Fred Oppenheimer's world to begin diplomatic relations with the first intelligent species we'd encountered.

"Did you ever watch Star Trek?" she asked.

"Yes, some. I didn't get into the television series, but I watched the movies with my dad."

"I loved it," she said. "That's part of why I am here. I wanted to help be a part of a peaceful scientific exploration of the universe. I always dreamed of that utopian, peaceful, and noble society. The adventure and wars and all of that didn't interest me, but it was the idea that we could ally ourselves with all of these different races on planets across the universe. It gave me hope. And here we are, about to begin that process. It isn't hyperbole to say that we were central players in one of the most important moments in human history. People will remember us forever, not just for finding the first intelligent being outside our own world, but for proving that the Chaos Machine is so much more than we ever thought. The advancements that will come from this trip will be astonishing and change how we interact with all of reality. An entire civilization will be established upon it. It will be based upon what we did here. Together. I am just giddy over how amazing it all is."

"I am too."

But I wasn't. Standing before the dawn of a new age of man may be some great privilege shared by only a handful of humans throughout time, but that awe was dwarfed by the looming heartbreak that would come when I would leave Kiersten forever.

"The Chaos Machine is intelligent," Kiersten continued, unaware of my turmoil. "That was an idea that had never really been explored, that we were creating a sentient being with this technology. When they trace back that discovery, they will see us. They will see how it pulled us together, then joined our planet with another planet. This moment will last forever."

"But we won't," I said, hating myself for letting my sorrow intrude on her joy.

Kiersten turned in my arms to face me. She took a moment to gaze into my eyes, her beautiful smile tempered with tenderness.

"I don't know what will happen after the jump," she began, leaning in close enough for our lips to touch. "But the Chaos Machine wants us together. It will find a way. I know it. It seems impossible right now, I know, but I've never been more certain of anything in my life. The Chaos Machine will hold us together. That is the end of our story, one that scientists and poets will recount until the end of time. That is what is truly great about this moment. Of all the things the Chaos Machine could have chosen to do, it chose to nurture our love and it will not stop when we get to Koi. I know this deep down to my core. Tell me that you believe me, Will. Even if just a little bit, even if just with a tiny piece of your heart, tell me that you believe that we are meant to be together and the Chaos Machine will find a way. Please, tell me, even if you have to lie to me, say that you believe."

"I believe."

***

We decided to make love during the jump. We never discussed a reason why or expressed a hope that it might somehow sway the Chaos Machine to bend reality to make our love a possibility. We just did and, for the first time in my life, everything seemed possible.

THE MARTIN & WEINKE CONTINUUM

From the escapades of a rock prophet to the global culling of humanity by Mother Nature, the Martin & Weinke Continuum connects standalone novels tracing our stumbling march to the end of civilization and beyond. These satirical, character-focused, and cross-genre stories examine our tenuous perch atop the food chain and what happens when everything else on the planet, both natural and unnatural, decides it's time for humans to be dethroned.

In order of continuity:

- *the dominant hand*
- *Deviants*
- *Pets*
- *How To Control Gravity and Other Stories*
- *Edward & The Island*
- *Edward & The Wilderness*
- *Edward & The Infinite*